WHAT'S THAT IN DOG YEARS?

illustrated by
julia christians

OXFORD
UNIVERSITY PRESS

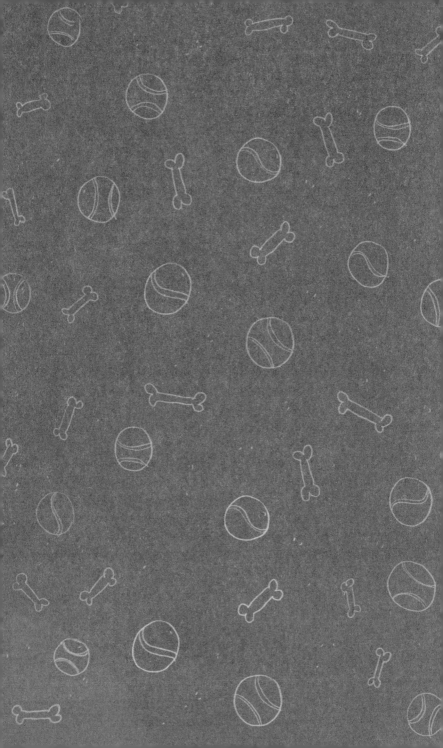

Chapter One

A sharp pebble pings off the back of my leg.

'Got him!' Tyler hoots. I hear him exchange a high five with his stupid friend, Ethan.

I keep my head down and ignore them. It's not the first time they've followed me after school but they normally get bored before now. I think what's done it today is they caught me writing an Ultra Boy and Wonder Dog story—based on me and my best mate Gizmo—and they think it's stupid and that I should take up their hobby of standing outside the Londis spitting at traffic.

'Going back to your Batcave, Batman?' one of them yells.

I say nothing. I wish I did have a Batcave. I'd just

stay down there all the time with Gizmo, working on scientific discoveries, like Everlasting Itch Powder that only works on people called Tyler and Ethan.

WHACK!

Ow! What was that? I touch the back of my head and wince. A half-eaten apple rolls past me.

That's it. Enough is enough. I take off and run to my house at the end of the cul-de-sac. I hear them behind me, still not giving up. I get my key out of my pocket. They'll regret messing with me. No more Mr Nice Guy.

You see, I have Gizmo well trained. Wait, that's not true, he's actually massively disobedient. But anyway, I have no doubt he will recognize that I'm in danger and will spring to my rescue with his teeth bared.

I throw the front door open, still dodging Ethan and Tyler's pebbles. They'll stop soon enough. Soon there will be the hammering of feet, a growl, and a leap through the air. Then they'll never mess with me again.

'Gizmo, get 'em!' I yell. And wait. And wait. And wait. What's going on? Where is he?

Tyler and Ethan laugh at me like I'm insane.

'Where's your dog, freakshow?' Ethan shouts.

I duck into the house. He isn't in the hall. That's weird. He always waits for me when I come home from school. I slam the door behind me and leave them to lob stuff at no one. I stick my head into the lounge. He's not in there either. He loves lying on the sofa, even though Mum complains he leaves hairs all over it. I call him again. Nothing. I go through to the kitchen. Oh. There he is, just having a lie-down.

'Gizmo!' I say. 'Wake up, I'm home.'

He opens his eyes but still doesn't move. He starts panting. This isn't right.

'Gizmo?' I say, shaking him. 'What's the matter, boy?'

He looks at me and tries to get up but he can't. I crouch next to him, trying to stop the panic rising in my chest. He's fine, he's fine. He's just tired. I shake him again. He groans a little and closes his eyes again. I run and grab a Jammie Dodger out of the tin and hold it in front of his nose. Jammie Dodgers are his favourite treat. He's not allowed them too often because they're not exactly healthy for dogs, but he has one when he's a good boy. I keep waving it but he doesn't even stir. No. Oh no. Tears prickle my eyes but I don't have time to cry. I have to get help. I call Mum but she doesn't answer. She never answers when she's at work. I stop for a moment and take a deep breath. I need to calm down for Gizmo. I'll be no help to him if I'm a wreck. I call Dad.

'Everything all right, George?' he slurs. I can tell from his voice he's only just woken up. He works nights so this is like first thing in the morning to him.

'No,' I say. 'Gizmo's not very well. He's not moving.'

He lets out one of those long Dad-breaths. 'Unnnnnngh. Are you sure he's not just asleep?'

'No,' I snap. 'He's not right. He's just lying there, not even responding to Jammie Dodgers. We need to get him to the vet's.'

Dad goes quiet. 'Can it not wait until your mum gets home?'

I stamp my feet like I'm four again. 'No. He's got to go now. Hurry.'

I hang up and wait. I google 'dog lying down, panting' but everything just seems to scream 'HE'S DYING'.

I sit next to Gizmo, stroking him. He can't go. Not now. He was fine this morning. How can things change so quickly?

I drag his bowl over and put it in front of his face. 'Drink. Drink. There's a good boy.'

He breathes out slowly through his nose and his eyelids flutter. I lie down and bury my face in his fur. I don't know how I'll cope if he dies now. He's been my best friend since I was born. Mum and Dad got him when he was a puppy and he's always been there. We've had adventures together in our Ultra Boy and Wonder Dog costumes, we've been on holiday together. When Mum and Dad split up, Gizmo was the only one I could talk to about it. I'm not ready for that to end.

Chapter Two

Gizmo is lying in my lap. He's awake now, but still not moving. God, I hate vets' waiting rooms. They smell like bleach and wet fur and pee and the walls are full of close-ups of deadly parasites. Dad taps my leg. He's holding a dog toy.

'Hey, Georgie,' he says. 'What's this?'

He moves it backwards and forwards in front of his mouth and goes, 'WOMP, WOMP, WOMP.'

I shrug and run my finger along the smooth patch on the back of Gizmo's left ear.

'A trom-*bone*,' says Dad, winking at me with a big grin on his face.

I groan. His jokes are always terrible but I especially don't need them here. The door opens and the vet calls us in. I carry Gizmo in and place him on the examination table. He raises his head slightly but that's it. This isn't right. He normally fights like hell to get off that table. And so would you if you associated it with having fingers jammed up your bum, I suppose.

The vet looks him over and does all kinds of tests on him. I stand in the corner, doing my finger exercises that help with my anxiety. Touch my index finger and thumb together, then my middle finger and thumb, then my third finger and thumb, then my little finger and thumb. Then start again on the other hand. When I was younger I had to go and see a therapist called Dr Kaur because of my panic attacks. Well, freakouts is what I call them. She taught me a few things that help me make them a bit better, but she couldn't stop me having them completely. I don't think anyone can do that.

Dad claps his hand on the back of my neck and squeezes, which startles me and I have to start again. I know he's trying to comfort me or whatever, but has he never heard of personal space?

'So,' says the vet, hanging her stethoscope around her neck. 'The good news is, it's just an infection which should clear up with antibiotics.'

I breathe a sigh of relief. The panic storm building in my head subsides to drizzle. At least it's nothing serious. But wait. She said, 'The good news is.' That is always followed by . . .

'The bad news is.'

I gulp. Here we go. The drizzle gets heavier. Before long it'll be a storm again. Maybe a hurricane. 'Gizmo is at an advanced age, and illnesses like this are going to become more frequent.'

'So what does that mean?' says Dad.

The vet pats Gizmo on the head. 'It means he might not have much more good quality life left,' she says. 'You should make the most of it.'

When we leave I'm in a daze. All of Dad's complaining about how expensive the antibiotics are fade into the background like white noise. I suppose I felt like Gizmo would go on for ever. I thought he'd always be there. Sure, he's slowed down a bit lately, but I thought he was just getting tired.

At home, I shut myself in my room with Gizmo. I can hear Mum and Dad in the living room arguing about who's paying for his treatment. I give Gizmo's back a scratch. He is already perking up a little bit.

'I can always rely on you to bring the family back

together, can't I, boy?'

I stick my earphones in and blast some music as loud as I can, then pull up my duvet and hide underneath it. I know Mum doesn't like me having Gizmo on my bed, but right now I don't care.

I nuzzle my nose into his scratchy fur and put my arms around him. I realize I've been taking things like this for granted. There'll only be so many snuggles, only so many walks. Life is precious. I have to make sure Gizmo has the best time possible. But what am I supposed to do? Hide him in a suitcase and take him to Florida to swim with dolphins? I need to get organized.

Nan is always going on about her 'bucket list'. Like, when she saw Tom Jones in concert and chucked her knickers at him, she said she could tick that one off her list. Old people are weird. But still, why can't I do something like that for Gizmo?

I lean across to my bedside table and pull out my notepad. I turn to a fresh page and in big black letters write, 'GIZMO'S BUCKET LIST'.

I'm thinking about all the things I want to do with Gizmo before he, you know, goes. What stuff does he *really* love?

'Hey, Gizmo,' I whisper, shutting the music off.

'You still like ice cream, right?'

Gizmo sits up, tilts his head, and licks his lips.

'Thought so. That can go on the list. How about going to a party? You like those, don't you?'

He tilts his head again, this time the other way. I'll take that as a yes. The last party he went to was our next door neighbours Mr and Mrs Clark's barbeque. He loved it. He stole Reverend Harris's hot dog and I overheard his wife call him a 'devil dog'.

I start writing a list, checking with him on every point. I can feel the worries of the vet and Mum and Dad STILL moaning at each other slip away. I just focus on all the good stuff me and Gizmo are going to do. Here's what I've got:

HAVE AN ICE CREAM

This one's a no-brainer. I mean technically he's not really supposed to eat them any more but one won't hurt.

GO TO A PARTY

Parties usually have two things: lots of people and lots of food. Two things Gizmo loves.

HAVE ONE MORE ULTRA BOY AND WONDER DOG ADVENTURE

Ultra Boy and Wonder Dog are two characters I invented, based on me and Gizmo. I write stories about them and the Intergalactic Power Squad.

We used to go off and have adventures based on my stories all the time and Gizmo loved it.

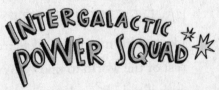

GET PAMPERED

Because all dogs deserve to be fussed over sometimes.

MAKE A CALENDAR

I've been meaning to do this for ages. You just take twelve photos, send them off, and they come back as a calendar. Gizmo loves dressing up and being centre of attention, so he'll enjoy it.

CLIMB THE BIG HILL ON THE OTHER SIDE OF TOWN

We've done this once before when I was really sad. I'd like to go back and make a happier memory.

GO CAMPING

Gizmo loves camping because he gets to eat loads of snacks, run around outside, and chase squirrels.

HAVE FIFTEEN MINUTES OF FAME

I know this might sound weird, but I just want the rest of the world to know how brilliant Gizmo is, even if only for a short time. I have no idea how I'm going to do this, but I'll try my best.

VISIT GOLDEN BEACH

The only time we ever took Gizmo on a proper holiday was to Golden Beach. He loved it. He ran on the sand, swam in the sea, and had loads of adventures. We would have been back before but, I don't know . . . things happened.

Getting there might be a bit tricky, too. Golden Beach is about two hundred miles away and there's no way I'll be able to afford the trip. And Mum and Dad? Forget it. Since Dad moved out, all they talk about is how tight money is. We don't have satellite TV at home any more, we don't shop as often, and when we do, it's at the cheap supermarket. Stuff for Gizmo is right at the bottom of the list of priorities. Plus, I've got a feeling neither of them will want to go back there. I'll have to work on it.

So I'm going to have to figure out a way to get enough money to get to Golden Beach. It seems impossible, but there's no way I *can't* do it.

I put down the notepad and Gizmo gives me a kiss. His breath smells like three-week-old beef, but I don't care. He is the best dog in the world.

Gizmo: A Dog's Tale

I'm getting on a bit now. I'm fourteen (that's roughly seventy-eight in dog years, you know) so I can't remember much about my young puppyhood. I know I was part of a litter and I know some humans took me away from my mum and my brothers and sisters, but other than that, it's a bit fuzzy. What I do know is, at some point, they abandoned me. I don't know why. Maybe I was too mad for them, maybe I was too funny-looking and not as cute as other dogs whose ears are the same size, or maybe they were just mean people. Whatever happened, they drove me to a car park and left me there in the rain. A nice lady in a van came and fetched me and took me to a big building filled with other dogs. It was noisy and smelly and scary. I was the smallest dog there.

After a while, a couple of big humans came to see me. The lady one smiled and cooed at me and said I was perfect. The man one said, 'I suppose he'll do.'

They took me to my new home. Everything was nice and clean. The big human lady was called Mum and the big human man was called Dad. They gave me a toy which they called Mr Monkey. He has been with me ever since. I can't sleep without him. He's looking a bit rough these days, and Mum has had to repair him more times than I can count, but he's still hanging in there. I had a lovely warm bed and plenty of food and cuddles. Mum and Dad treated me like a king. Sadly, it didn't last too long. Mum started getting round and they spent more time buying things and putting them in the other bedroom than they did playing with me. It seemed like my time as the centre of attention would be short. I was sad for a while. But when they brought the tiny human home, everything changed. He was smaller than me but louder than ten of me. He pooped way more than me, too. But he didn't stay tiny for long. Soon, he was walking around and coming straight for me. He would hug me and kiss me and share his Jammie Dodgers with me. It wasn't long until we were best friends. His name is George.

When he has a bad day, he tells me all about it, and I make him feel better just by being next to him. When he has one of his freakouts, I'm the only one that can calm him down.

His vet told him that he should write to clear his head, too, and that is his main hobby. He writes stories about Ultra Boy and Wonder Dog, a crime-fighting duo who are part of the Intergalactic Power Squad. When he draws pictures of them, they kind of look like the two of us.

I enjoy hearing the stories and snoozing next to him on the bed while he writes them. They keep him going when things are tough, like when Dad left. That was a sad time for everyone, but we got through it because we are a team. We are the Intergalactic Power Squad!

Chapter Three

I meet my best (human) friend Matt in Form. He used to call for me, but stopped a few months ago. He reckons he needs more time to do his hair in the morning. I don't know why. It looks like two hedgehogs have waddled onto his head and died. I tell him everything that happened with Gizmo, but he doesn't seem that interested. He's all, 'Yeah. Hmm. That's mad.' And the whole time, he never looks up from his phone. Probably messaging the rest of 'the ManDem', the group chat he set up with Ethan and Tyler.

That's right, my so-called best friend is mates with my sworn enemies. I hadn't properly had it out with him before today, but enough's enough. I mean, they literally chased me down the street and tried to concuss me with fruit.

'So Matt,' I say. 'You're my mate, yeah?'

He huffs and rolls his eyes. 'What are you on about?'

'And you're mates with Ethan and Tyler, too?'

He finally puts his phone on standby and looks at me. 'So?'

I didn't know what to say. How do you explain something so obvious?

'Well, we've been best mates since we were five, right?' I say. 'So maybe it's a bad idea for you to be friends with people who, you know, make my life a misery.'

Matt picks his phone back up and slumps down in his seat. 'I've told you before, I'm not getting involved in your beefs.'

I want to tell him how sick-makingly insane that is, but our form teacher Mr Brandrick strides in and you don't want to annoy him because he's a PE teacher and he'll make you do laps. Yes, even in a classroom.

'Listen up, you little berks,' Mr Brandrick

booms. 'I have a missive from the Head which is as follows: Woodlet High has been chosen to participate in the UK Educational Video Challenge.' He pauses as if he's expecting us all to go, 'Oooooooooh', but I've never heard of it and I'm pretty sure no one else has either.

'Anyway,' he goes on, pushing his glasses onto the top of his head and squinting at a piece of paper. 'The idea is, you make a video about an educational subject and the best one from the school goes through to the final and the best one from that goes on telly.' Mr Brandrick throws the paper down. 'You all know what telly is, right? It's the thing we used to watch before you got your MeTubes and your SnappySnaps and what have you.'

Matt sticks up his hand.

'What is it, Copeland?' Mr Brandrick says.

'Do we have to do it?'

Most of the class laughs, but I don't. It sounds like loads of fun and who knows? This could be the thing that gets Gizmo his fifteen minutes of fame.

'Yes, you do,' says Mr Brandrick. 'The Head is keen that everyone takes part so we stand a better chance of winning. The school could do with the good publicity.'

I don't know why. Last time an inspector was here, they reckoned the school was so good, it needed 'special measures'.

'Quite frankly, the entire thing is a pain in the proverbial, but an order's an order, so I'm going to need your videos in by the end of the week.' A groan ripples around the room, but I'm delighted. I mean, it's a lot better than the usual homework we get.

'QUIET WHILE I'M TALKING!' Mr Brandrick snaps. 'Now I would have given you more notice, but it rather slipped my mind, what with me being preoccupied with piffling things like quality education.'

I involuntarily laugh and Brandrick shoots me a look like he wants to karate chop my skull off. 'Anyway, work in your pairs. Make it quick and make it educational. If I have to watch any nonsense to do with dabbering or Nitecraft, I will put you in detention until the Rapture, do you understand me?'

I glance at Matt to see when he's up for starting our video but he's too busy secretly texting under the table. Never mind, we'll sort it out later. We don't do as much stuff together as we used to, so this is going to be fun. Loads of fun.

Matt

I first met Matt when George was small. Even though he was stealing my best friend, I still liked him. He used to bring me biscuits from his house which were delicious.

George was already writing Ultra Boy and Wonder Dog stories by then and added a new character: AntiMatter Kid. That was Matt. The three of us used to travel the galaxy (the back garden) and bring down bad guys together. Well, George tried to teach me to bring bad guys down, but I'd never do it. I'm too nice.

One year at Christmas (one of my favourite times of year because I get a stocking and lots of leftover turkey), Auntie Gloria made Ultra Boy, Wonder Dog, and AntiMatter Kid costumes for us and we wore them all the time.

One of my favourite memories is from when George was at little school. They had some kind of costume day and we all wore our outfits. They even let me come in for the morning. They soon regretted this. After they brought me to the front of the class and we demonstrated our superpowers, the teacher asked me to sit quietly at the back. The thing about me is, sitting quietly isn't really my thing. Especially in those days. It was a hot day and the door was propped open. A delicious smell wafted in from the kitchen. I have an incredible nose so I knew straight away it was burgers, my favourite food in the universe, besides Jammie Dodgers. While everyone was distracted, I sneaked out of the classroom and followed the scent. I crept past a class in the big hall and pushed my way into the kitchen. That was where I saw a tray of delicious, juicy burgers on the counter.

Luckily for me, there was a trolley nearby, so I hopped up on that and from there it was an easy step onto the counter and the best burgers I've ever had in my life. I'd wolfed down six of them before a lady with a net on her hair screamed, 'A rat! A giant rat!'

George got in so much trouble for that, but after the teachers had finished telling him off, he and Matt laughed so much. It was the funniest thing to have ever happened at school. When he got home, Mum and Dad told him off again, but when they weren't looking, he stroked my fur and giggled and kissed me, saying I was the best. George and Matt talked about that day for years afterwards, telling everyone they met.

I don't see Matt so much these days. When he does come over, he doesn't play with me. He just sits there looking moody. I don't know what's got into him, but I hope he comes around soon. The Intergalactic Power Squad needs AntiMatter Kid.

Chapter Four

Mum is back when I get home. Some days she finishes early. After forcing one of her trademark Mum cheek-kisses on me, she tells me what she has planned for Gizmo.

'A whole new diet regime.' She spreads her arms like she's revealing the grand finale to a magic trick. 'I've been reading about it online. They say you can make your dog healthier by ditching processed foods and switching to pure meat and veg. And get this: it works out cheaper.'

I glance at Gizmo, his chin resting on Mr Monkey. He does not look impressed. Jammie Dodgers are basically his entire reason to live.

'In fact, I think all of us would benefit from a switch to a healthier diet,' Mum goes on.

Ah great. Everything's getting worse.

Mum motions for me to sit down and plonks a cup of tea on the table. She sits opposite with her 'I Wish This Was Prosecco' mug and blows her steaming-hot black coffee.

'So,' she says. 'How was your day?'

This is the ritual, now. Since Dad left, we seem to have started loads of them. We now have a set mealtime, which always takes place around the table. No more balancing plates on our laps in front of the telly. And there's a colour-coded chores rota stuck to the fridge door. And we always have to sit down and talk about my day at school. You could set your watch to it.

'Fine,' I say, my standard answer even when I've had a horrible day.

'Just fine?' says Mum. 'You know your school days are the best days of your life, don't you?'

Ugh. I hope not. Gizmo slurps water from his bowl noisily then comes over for a fuss.

'Actually Mum,' I say, 'I do have something I could do with asking you.'

Mum hastily swallows her coffee and clasps her

hands together. 'OK, George, I am an open book. You can ask me anything. You are growing up and becoming a man, after all.'

'Blurgh! No, it's not about that!' I yell. And let's be honest, if I have questions about puberty, there's no way I'm ever going to Mum. What does she think Wikipedia is for?

'Well what is it, then?'

I scratch behind Gizmo's ear. I'd been thinking about this video and what we could do for it. It needs to be something really good, and it needs to involve Gizmo in some way.

'Do you think I'd be able to teach Gizmo some tricks?'

Mum looks confused. 'What kind of tricks?'

'Oh, you know, rolling over, playing dead, dancing, that kind of thing.'

Mum chuckles. 'I don't know, but if you could teach him how to work a washing machine, it would be a huge help.'

I hardly think the judges of the UK Educational Video thingy would be interested in watching a dog washing some pants, but I don't say anything. I decide to do what I always do when I want to learn something, and head to YouTube.

I go up to my room with Gizmo, pull out the laptop, and after waiting approximately eight million years for the old thing to load up, search for dog training videos. I'm not sure how I'm going to make Gizmo doing loads of tricks into an educational thing, but I'll figure it out. Maybe I'll dress him as a Roman centurion or something.

Anyway, the top result is this bloke called Juan Hernandez—The Dog Fixer. He's got tons of views so he must be good. I click on a video and position it so both me and Gizmo can see it.

When it loads up, Juan, whose teeth are the whitest things I've ever seen in my life, grins at the camera and says, 'Hi there dog lovers, I'm Juan Hernandez and in this video, I'm going to show you how to teach your dog to roll over.'

I glance at Gizmo. The only time he ever rolled over was when he chased a squirrel down a bank but went too fast and ended up doing a massive cartwheel into some stingers.

'OK, so what you have to do first is encourage your dog to get on its side, like so.'

Juan crouches down next to an immaculate white poodle. Gizmo is a Border terrier crossed with something, we don't know what. He's small and his fur is light brown and scratchy like the rough side of a sponge. There are flecks of grey in his muzzle and he has one ear bigger than the other. The dog in this video is like the anti-Gizmo. Juan touches its nose, then its shoulder, and it lies down on its side.

'Good girl, Persephone,' he says, grinning so wide I nearly go snow-blind. Then he touches her other shoulder and she rolls fully over, before jumping up and yipping. Juan strokes her head and gives her a little biscuit.

'Positive reinforcement is key,' says Juan. 'Give your buddy a treat when they do good. Now it's time for you to try. Let's get rollin'!'

I look at Gizmo. He stares back at me as if to say, 'Yeah jog on, mate.'

I touch his nose, then his shoulder. He blinks slowly and yawns. Hmm. I'm going to need some of that positive reinforcement Juan was going on about.

We run downstairs and I open Gizmo's treat tin. Empty. Now, I knew Mum wasn't buying any new Jammie Dodgers, but I wasn't expecting her to get rid of the old ones.

'I gave them to Mrs Hassan for her Reginald,' Mum says, smiling as she chops what look like weeds.

Gizmo growls under his breath. Reginald, the King Charles spaniel from across the road is his arch-enemy. The Darth Vader to his Luke Skywalker. They've got some serious history.

Reginald

Ah, my oldest foe. The two of us have never seen eye to eye. Ever since he showed up, he's had a problem with me. He sits in that window all day and when I walk past with George, he can't help but stick his oar in. Always got something to say.

It all came to a head one day in the park. He was there with his human and I was with mine. George was throwing a stick for me and I was fetching it and bringing it back, which is easily one of my top five favourite things to do.

1. Fetching sticks.
1. Eating Jammie Dodgers.
1. Snuggling with Mr Monkey.
1. Chasing squirrels.
1. Playing with George.

Notice how they're all number one? That's because I can't possibly put them in order.

So we were at the park and I was going for the stick. I could almost taste the sweet, sweet bark in my mouth, when suddenly, like a bolt of black and white lightning, Reginald swooped in and snatched it up. No way. That was mine. Well, I went after him quick as I could and we rolled down the hill like a bowling ball made of canine hatred.

Ever since then, we've been sworn enemies. Come for my stick and feel my wrath.

'So what is he supposed to have for treats?' I ask
Mum, putting the lid back on the empty tub.

Mum opens the fridge and chucks a bag at me.
'Carrot sticks. Healthy *and* tasty.'

I can't believe what I'm seeing. 'But he's a dog,
not a rabbit.'

Mum laughs. 'He'll love them, I promise.'

We'll see. I open the bag and take out one of the
sticks. It feels as cold and dry as one of Nan's kisses.
'Here you go.' I hold it out for Gizmo to take. He
sniffs it for a second, then decides he'd rather chew
his own bum.

'See?'

'He'll get used to it,' says Mum. 'He'll have to.
No more sugary treats for you, my little man.'

I sigh. There's no way I'll get Gizmo doing tricks
like this. I know they say you need to dangle a carrot
sometimes, but I don't think they mean it literally.
Wait a second. I root around in my pocket and in
amongst the lint, bent paperclips, and tiny balls of
paper is fifty pence. Ah ha! While Mum is distracted
starting dinner, I sneak out and run to the shop at
the top of the road. The only thing I can find for that
money is a big cookie that passes its sell-by date
today. That'll do. I buy it and take Gizmo onto the

back lawn for another attempt. I break off a small piece and encourage him to lie down on the grass.

He watches the tiny piece of cookie like it's the most valuable treasure in the world. He licks his lips but it's not enough to stop the Gizmo trademark drool string.

'OK,' I say, glancing over my shoulder to make sure Mum can't see the illegal biscuit. 'Now, are you going to roll over for me, Gizmo?'

Gizmo leans over slightly. He's doing it! He's really doing it! Fourteen years old and doing new stuff. That's roughly seventy-eight in dog years. You don't see many seventy-eight-year-old humans rolling over, do you? I start clapping and cheering him on, but he quickly flips back upright, snatches the cookie off the floor, and takes off across the lawn. I try to stop him, but the sweet treat is already gone. He barely even chewed it. Maybe this isn't going to be as easy as I thought.

'Dinner time, boys,' Mum calls from the kitchen, bang on schedule. 'We're having tofu casserole.'

Me and Gizmo look at each other. Then he hides behind the bin. I think I'll join him.

Chapter Five

I've been reminding Matt all day about the video.
I've decided we'll just have to wing it. Gizmo is the
funniest dog ever and we've had loads of fun as a trio.
There's no way we won't make a great video. Easily
better than anything the stupid ManDem could come
up with. What could they educate anybody about,
anyway? How to have less intelligence than a
turnip and still manage to tie your shoelaces?

We're walking to mine. Matt isn't
talking much, just staring at his phone.

'What are you laughing at?' I ask him.

He shakes his head. 'Ah, you wouldn't get it.'

'No, go on,' I say. I just want to be involved in
his jokes. His sense of humour has changed since

we moved up to high school. We used to laugh ourselves stupid over fart jokes, but now it's different. I can't figure out how exactly.

Matt huffs and shows me his phone. It's a photo of Henry Mason from our year with his mouth open. It looks like he's mid-word in a conversation and someone's taken a photo without telling him. In bold white meme lettering at the bottom, it says, 'wat'.

I smile a bit, but I'm bad at faking laughter.

'Told you you wouldn't get it,' he says, yanking his phone back.

'Pretty sure I do,' I say. 'You're making fun of Henry.'

Matt laughs and kicks a pebble at a bin. 'What's wrong with that?'

We turn onto my street. Mrs Hassan is taking Reginald out for a walk. We have an unspoken arrangement to go at different times.

'Just a bit mean, that's all.'

Matt laughs harder and squeezes my cheek. 'You're adorable, Georgie Boy.'

When we go inside, Gizmo comes skittering down the hall, his big ear flapping behind him and his tongue hanging out of the side of his mouth. He always greets me like this. It's as if he's overjoyed that I've actually come home. Maybe when you're abandoned at an early age it affects you for the rest of your life.

He jumps up my legs and I bend over to fuss him and let him kiss me all over my face. Some people say that it's disgusting for your dog to do that because you don't know where their tongue has been, but come on. I don't know where Auntie Gloria's been but I'm supposed to let her kiss me on the cheek whenever I see her. When he's finished with me, he hops over to Matt, who lightly touches his head, then steps away. Gizmo gives me a look as if to say, 'What's his problem?' I just shrug.

We head out to the back garden to start shooting our video. I know better than to do it in the living room because we'd probably end up breaking an ornament and Mum would go insane.

Our back garden is looking kind of sad these days. Dad was the only keen gardener in the family so the flowers are mostly dead and the mini greenhouse is empty. Our barbeque is sitting there getting wet from a mixture of rain and Gizmo's wee. That used to be Dad's pride and joy—the Grillmaster XLK8000. He reckoned it had more dials and settings than one of the rockets that went to the moon. When we had parties, the area around it would be Dad's kingdom. He'd stand next to it in his 'funny' muscleman apron and never leave all night, serving up burgers, sausages, kebabs, some kind of exotic Mongolian stew. It was his favourite toy and I bet he would have taken it with him if he hadn't moved into a flat. Since he left, we've only tried using it once. Mum couldn't figure it out though and ended up kicking it and ordering a Chinese.

Matt stays on the patio because he doesn't want to get any mud on his trainers. He's really into trainers now. I remember a time when he just saw them as something which kept you from hurting your feet on pointy stones, but now they're more important than oxygen. They're bright red with thin white stripes running along the side. When I told him I thought they looked a bit stupid, he didn't speak to me for three days.

'So I thought for the video, we could get around the educational thing by setting it at school,' I say.

Matt groans. 'Can't we just do a couple of sums or read out of a book and get it over with quick? I've got places to be.'

Places to be? What places? You know what, forget the places. Try and keep him here. Think of something he'll like.

'We could do impressions of teachers!' I say. 'And we could have them saying educational stuff so it fits the bill.'

He smiles a little. I knew he'd be into that. It's making fun of people, his favourite thing in the world, apparently.

'All right, but I don't want to be on camera,' he says, because of course he doesn't. Since he's started hanging out with Ethan and Tyler, it seems like it's become illegal for him to actually get enthusiastic about anything that isn't his stupid red trainers. You could drive up to his house with a truck full of twenty-pound notes and he probably wouldn't even bother to answer the door.

'Well, we don't have to,' I say. 'We'll just dress Gizmo up and do voices off-camera so it looks like he's talking.'

Matt splutters with laughter. 'All right, you're on.'

Turning him into Mr Brandrick is pretty easy. I find an old baseball cap and put it on the smallest setting. Then I print off a photo of a tracksuit top, stick it onto some card from a cereal box, and attach it to Gizmo's collar. When Matt sees it, he laughs until he almost cries. I can't remember the last time I made that happen. While we start filming on his phone, he's shaking so much, I'm pretty sure the picture will be wobbling all over the place.

'Listen up, you 'orrible bunch of brain-dead zombies,' I yell in a voice that sounds kind of like Mr Brandrick, but not really. 'If you don't drop and give me twenty this instant, I am going to punt a rugby ball right in your face.' What makes it funnier is Gizmo's standard dopey expression being a complete contrast to what he's saying.

Next, I put a tie on Gizmo and film while Matt does his impression of our Geography teacher, Mr Marshall. 'Pens down, pleeeaaasse,' he drones. 'If I have to arrrrrssskkk again, I will become very annoooooooyyed.'

We keep going for ages and by the time we're finished, we've done four teachers each. My face hurts from laughing so much.

'I reckon we stand a good chance, don't you?' I ask Matt.

'Definitely,' he replies, wiping tears from his eyes. 'This was loads of fun.'

We arrange for him to send the videos over so I can edit them together in time for tomorrow. His camera is better than mine so they should be good quality.

When Matt leaves and I sit down at exactly six-fifteen for dinner and a discussion of how my day has been, for the first time in for ever, I don't have to lie. Today actually *has* been fine. I feel like I'm getting my friend back.

I'm walking Gizmo when I get a text.

Actually mate. I might as well edit the video.

I nearly fall over. Matt is into something! And it's with me! Today has been more than fine. It's been incredible!

Dressing Up

You probably think most dogs hate dressing up, don't you? Well I'm not like most dogs. Over the course of my seventy-eight dog years, I have dressed up as the following:

- 🐕 Wonder Dog (obviously).
- 🐕 A bee.
- 🐕 A dragon.
- 🐕 An elf.
- 🐕 Some teachers from George's school.

And probably loads more I have forgotten about. But my favourite costume of all time has to be the one the vet put on me after I had an operation. It was a large, plastic cone around my neck. I caused SO MUCH MISCHIEF in that! People would be standing around, minding their own business when WHACK! Here comes Gizmo!

This happened around the time of the human festival of Halloween—probably my favourite of the human holidays. It's the one day of the year when humans act like dogs: they perform for treats.

We were supposed to be dressing as the

Intergalactic Power Squad that year, but George didn't think Wonder Dog would be seen dead wearing that cone, so they had a last-minute rethink. George put on face paint, a wig, and a tail and became the MGM lion, Matt wore white and carried a fishing rod so he could be the DreamWorks boy, and I was the Pixar desk lamp. We earned so many sweets that night.

Chapter Six

We're sitting in Form and Mr Brandrick has all the videos queued up on the computer. Ours is fourth. My heart pounds and I start to sweat but it's OK, because it's not like my freakouts. It's butterflies in my stomach. Kind of a nice feeling. Anxiety isn't butterflies. It's bloodthirsty pterodactyls.

'OK, let's not prolong this nonsense,' says Mr Brandrick. 'We'll all vote at the end for the two winners and they'll go through to the next round and so on and so forth. But if they cross the line, and I mean even by a fraction of a millimetre—I'm talking a gnat's eyelash—I will disqualify them.'

I gulp. I hope ours hasn't crossed the line. Even if it has, it's so funny, there's no way he can keep it out. I could hardly sleep last night because I kept remembering random bits and giggling to myself.

The first video is just Raj Thakrar and Amy Stanford reading from a science textbook. No competition there. The second video is Sammy James and Jack Fox having a really boring French conversation. Now I'm beginning to think we've got this in the bag. I try to make eye contact with Matt but he's just staring straight ahead.

The third one is slightly better: it's Josh Callaghan and Ade Alli doing sock puppets based on Shakespeare. They're getting pretty good laughs but then one of the socks says a mildly rude word and Mr Brandrick roars, 'CROSSED THE LINE—DISQUALIFIED!'

I nudge Matt but he still doesn't respond.

'All right, after that travesty, let's move onto Duggan and Copeland's offering.' He presses play on our video and the butterflies go hyper. I can't wait for everyone to see our video and how funny Gizmo is.

The screen flickers into life. Wait a second. There must be some mistake. Why is there a piece of paper on the screen? I stick my hand up.

'Sir, I think you're playing the wrong video.'

Mr Brandrick glares at me like he wants to strangle me and Matt kicks my shin under the table. A hand holding a pen appears and starts writing numbers. Then a low, flat voice starts. 'Two plus two equals four. Four plus four equals eight.'

Wait a second. That's Matt's voice! 'What's this all about?' I whisper, but he doesn't answer. The video finishes on the grand finale of ten plus ten equals twenty before cutting off.

'Well,' Mr Brandrick growls. 'Just when I thought I'd witnessed the lowest effort put into a piece of schoolwork, I discover previously uncharted depths.' He shakes his head. 'Pathetic. And why weren't you in it, Duggan?'

I try to explain that I *was* in it but he cuts me off with a raised hand and a, 'Ahhhhbababababa.' Here we go. 'If my detentions weren't already packed past fire safety regulations, I would be adding you this instant. Right, onto the next Oscar-worthy production...'

When we leave class, I finally manage to grab Matt. 'What was all that about?'

He shakes his head like I'm bothering him. 'The videos didn't work when I tried to edit them together. The files were corrupted. Any more questions?'

Yes, I do have more questions, but they're mostly variations on, 'Why do you think I'd be so stupid to believe that pile of dog slop?' But before I can say anything, he's already seen Tyler and Ethan on the other side of the corridor and is strutting over.

He knew exactly what he was doing, I'm sure of it.

Walkies

I don't always hear the humans when they talk to me.
Phrases like 'bath time' and 'bedtime' and 'Gizmo,
stop eating my socks' are often said too quietly for
me to understand. But there's one word I never miss,
even if it's being whispered into a pillow fifty miles
away.

WALKIES!

As soon as I hear that magic word, I stop
whatever I'm doing, jump up, and run for the door
like it's made of Meaty Schmackos. George keeps
my lead in the kitchen on a hook he made at school.
It has a stick drawing of a dog and it says, 'Gizmoe'.
His spelling wasn't the greatest back then.

Walkies have changed a lot over the years. It
used to be me and Mum and Dad, then before George
could do his own walkies (it takes humans a long
time to figure it out) they added a pram to the mix.
After that, it would be George with either Mum or
Dad, and then just George.

These days, typical walkies go something like
this:

1. George puts on my lead.

2. I say goodbye to Mr Monkey.

3. We leave the house and turn right up the street.

4. That scoundrel Reginald talks trash at me from his windowsill and I give back as good as I get.

5. I stop at my favourite lamp post and sniff to check that none of the other dogs in the neighbourhood have claimed it. I have a nice lengthy wee on it to take it back in the name of Gizmo.

6. We go to the park and George throws a stick for me.

7. I fetch it for him and he throws it again. Repeat until I have to lie down.

8. I might throw in something special here. It might be chasing a squirrel so it has to hide up a tree, it might be rolling around in mud, it might be having a play-fight with my old mate Benji the Labrador. On a warm day, I might just dive straight in the lake.

9. Head home for dinner. I used to prefer this bit
   before Mum started feeding me rabbit food.

Our walkies aren't always the same, though.
We sometimes go on special ones. Like the time we
climbed the biggest hill in town. That was tiring
but fun. What happened before that wasn't fun but
maybe we'll talk about that later.

So that's walkies. One of my favourite things in
the entire world.

Chapter Seven

When I get home today I receive a text from Matt.

Soz about video.

I text back straight away.

Sorry because it didn't work or sorry because it did and you didn't want to show it, for some reason?

He hasn't replied yet. God, why are humans so complicated? I snuggle next to Gizmo on the sofa with the laptop while he reluctantly nibbles at a low-fat veggie chew. I google 'Things to do with dogs near me'. If Matt is going to be weird, I might as well do more stuff with Gizmo. Plus, I really need to crack on with the bucket list. I still haven't ticked anything off it yet. The first hit is a local forum called Tammerstone Dog Lovers. Hmm. I didn't know there were actual organized groups for this kind of thing.

There are loads of posts about good walks for dogs in the area, but I'm pretty sure I know all of them. Then something catches my eye near the bottom of the page.

Tammerstone Cross-Breed Dog Show
Sunday 24th June. The best non-pedigree event in town! Prize for Best in Show—£400.

Four hundred quid. That's easily enough to get us to Golden Beach. I click on the link and read on:

Judges will be looking for the best cross-breed dog around, so if your furry friend is obedient and has a few tricks in their repertoire, come on down.

Ugh. I knew there'd be a catch. Gizmo isn't exactly what you'd call obedient. And we saw what happened when I tried to teach him tricks. Still, I can't get that money out of my mind. Maybe there's some way I can get Gizmo doing tricks. A few basic ones might be enough.

The door opens and Mum walks in. She does that, 'oooooh oooh,' doorbell noise she always does, then hangs her bag up, and flops down in the chair. She looks tired. She looks tired a lot lately.

'Hello George,' she says, heavy-lidded and soft. Gizmo trots over and nudges her dangling hand for a fuss. 'And hello Gizmo.' She raises her eyebrows at me. 'Did you know I caught this beast trying to eat my tights this morning? If I hadn't walked in when I did he'd be doing some very interesting poos over the next twenty-four hours.'

Ugh. I love Gizmo but he can be really grim sometimes.

Mum stretches and yawns. 'Make yourself useful and stick the kettle on, will you? I'm spitting feathers.'

I go into the kitchen and start making tea. I check the chores rota. Oh no. My day to do the bins. I take Mum's cup of tea in to her and then drag the horrible bin bag out to the wheelie. When I turn around, Gizmo is standing right behind me, wagging his tail. While we're out here, maybe we could try and do some tricks? All it will take is a bit of practice, I'm sure of it. We go onto the lawn. It's not muddy at all; I don't know why Matt thought it would ruin his precious red trainers.

'Gizmo!' I say. 'Sit!'

He sniffs at a patch on the ground then goes on his haunches and starts pooing.

'That's not what I said!'

After he's finally finished doing his business and I've bagged it up and binned it, I go back to try again. 'Gizmo, sit!' He doesn't sit. Maybe there's something wrong with his ears. I should test them. I take three steps back and whisper, 'Dinner'. He spins around and runs straight into the kitchen. Yeah, there's nothing wrong with his hearing.

I get my phone out and google 'Dog training Tammerstone'. There has to be some way of getting him to listen. The top result is: 'Dog Obedience Training—Guaranteed Results.' Hmm. I click on it.

Practically Pawfect Dog Centre
OBEDIENCE—GROOMING—BOARDING

This place looks pretty smart. I bet they could sort Gizmo out and get him ready for that show, no problem. I'll have to check them out.

'George!' Mum shouts from the kitchen. 'When you empty the bin, replace the bag!'

Chapter Eight

Man, this new diet is miserable. The way I see it, if God had intended us to eat stuff that grows out of the ground, he wouldn't have made it taste so disgusting. Plus, I feel like it's damaging my insides. I don't want to get too graphic, but my farts could fell a buffalo.

Another thing that's miserable is wet break times. I used to spend them in the classroom with Matt, just chatting and writing Intergalactic Power Squad stories. Today, I'm writing alone while Matt, Tyler, and Ethan crowd around the table next to me.

Any hope I have of concentrating on what I'm doing is dashed when Tyler starts playing grime music through some rubbish wireless speakers.

'Aw, sick,' says Ethan.

'Yeah man, sick,' Matt agrees, even though just a few months ago he said he hated grime and even went to a Little Mix concert with his mum and sisters.

'What do you think, dogboy?' says Tyler.

I ignore him. I wish I could turn into a dog on command, though. Supposed to be playing rugby? Sorry, can't do it, I'm a dog. Mum wants me to watch one of those rubbish old films she loves? Nope. Dog. Chemistry homework due tomorrow? What do you know? I ate it because I'm a dog.

A ball of paper hits me on the side of the head. 'He asked you a question,' says Ethan.

I look at Matt. He just stares straight ahead, not encouraging them, but not sticking up for me either. Standard procedure.

'I think it's the worst thing I've ever heard,' I say.

When I first started here, I pretended to like Ethan and Tyler in the hope that they'd at least leave me alone. Needless to say, it didn't work, so now I don't bother.

They laugh and nudge each other like they're doing some kind of orangutan mating ritual.

'That's a shame,' says Tyler, 'because we were going to invite you to a party Saturday night.'

Now I've heard everything. 'Oh really?' I say, not even looking up from my pad.

'Yeah,' says Ethan. 'It's at Casey Marshall's house. Fancy dress.'

I stop and think for a second. Maybe a fancy dress party could be a good way to tick something off Gizmo's list.

'Is this for real?' I ask Matt.

'Course it is,' he says, still not looking at me.

'Who are you going as?' I ask him.

He shrugs. 'Cowboy? So are you coming, or what?'

I don't know whether it's a good idea or not but I find myself agreeing. Maybe Matt and I could have fun there like we did at my house the other day.

'Could I take Gizmo?' I ask, thinking about the list.

Tyler and Ethan laugh but Matt nudges them and shakes his head. 'Course,' he says, smiling. 'The more the merrier.'

I consider it some more. This could be horrible. Then again, it could be brilliant.

'OK, we'll go.'

'Cool,' says Matt. 'I'll text you the address.'

Tyler changes the song on his phone to an even worse one, but I don't mind. I'm already planning how the party is going to go. I'll keep Matt away from Tyler and Ethan, remind him of how amazingly fun Gizmo and I are, and things will be back to normal. Easy.

Chapter Nine

Wow, Practically Pawfect is posh. It looks like
Hogwarts. Actually, Dogwarts. They should have
called it that. It's on the grounds
of a big country house that
has a fancy shopping centre—
there's a place that sells expensive
candles, a wine cellar, and a cheese shop, all in these
converted barns. You have to walk past them to get
to the dog place, which is set a little way back in
some vast green parkland.

I get Gizmo on a short lead and go inside.
Everything is white and pristine. It seems too clean
for a place that has dogs in it. At the desk, a sign tells
me to ding the bell for attention, so I do it. A lady

about Mum's age comes out of a room just behind. 'Can I help you?'

'Um, yes,' I say. 'I was wondering if I could sign my dog up for obedience classes?'

She peers over the desk at Gizmo and raises her eyebrows. I notice a badge on her cardigan that says 'Margaret'. 'OK. Well, our one-month programmes start at three hundred pounds.'

THREE HUNDRED QUID? Do they teach them to do your homework for you or something?

'Um, is there a cheaper one?'

The lady's mouth twists into a smirk. 'Maybe. But not here.'

I slump outside, back onto the gravel. I reach down and tickle Gizmo's ear. 'We don't need their snooty class anyway do we, boy?'

The problem is, we kind of do. Winning that show is the only way I'll ever be able to get enough money to get to Golden Beach. And we really need to get to Golden Beach. There's no way we're winning it at our current level of ability. I'm going to have to think of something else.

I'm about to turn around and head home when a couple of expensive cars pull in. These are even fancier than the ones already parked up. Wow. You never see anything like that down my way. No scratches, no eyelashes, or 'Princess on Board' bumper stickers. A bloke gets out of the first car and lets out a Labrador with the shiniest coat you've ever seen in your life. A woman holding a chihuahua the size of a guinea pig trots out of the other one. I bet they're here for the obedience class. The bloke goes to a 'Members Only' gate at the side of the main building and holds his keys up against a black panel which makes it open. Wait a second. Maybe I could take a peek. Just to see what it's like. I hurry Gizmo across the car park and get behind the lady and the chihuahua. She opens the gate, and seeing me behind, holds it for me. Here we go: we're in.

I follow them down a passage until we arrive at a patio at the back of the building. All around us are what look like old stables that have been converted into proper buildings. Maybe it's where they board the dogs. Gizmo stops and has a good long sniff at a stone lion statue.

'Get a load of that, Gizmo,' I say. 'Posh dog wee. I bet it smells nicer than what you're used to.'

A few dogs and their owners have congregated in the middle of the patio. As well as the Labrador and the chihuahua, there is a Dalmatian, a corgi, and a beagle. Not a cross in sight.

'Play it cool, boy,' I mutter through the side of my mouth. 'As far as these people know, we belong here.'

He seems to take in what I say but then immediately cocks his leg and does a massive wee up the lion. I guess that's his way of showing he belongs. When he's done, I lead him towards the centre of the group. The key is to not look like an outsider.

'We've been feeding Bullion organic kelp and activated almonds,' says the Dalmatian's owner.

'Yes I tried that with Zirconia,' says the chihuahua lady. 'But she prefers quinoa and venison.'

For all I know, quinoa and venison are the names of two other dogs, but I don't say anything.

The corgi owner, an old bloke with eyebrows like two retired caterpillars, looks at us. 'I don't think I've seen you before. What's this fellow's name?'

I gulp. They're all staring at me. I feel like a chimney sweep gatecrashing a royal wedding. I think about making up a name, telling them he's called Lord Cyril Fancyford and I feed him discombobulated apricots, but my brain can't work quickly enough and I just say, 'Gizmo.'

'And what . . . is Gizmo?' the beagle's owner asks me, squinting at him like he's a tricky crossword.

I shrug. 'A dog?'

They all laugh and my face goes as red as the Ferrari in the car park. Think before you speak, idiot.

'I meant what breed?' he asks.

'Oh,' I say. 'Well, he's a rescue so we don't know. My mum says he's half Border terrier, half Satan.' I laugh, but the others just smile a bit. I'm not sure, but it looks like Zirconia the chihuahua's owner pulls her away slightly.

A door at the back of the main building swings open and a woman jogs out. She's wearing a powder-blue tracksuit and box-fresh white trainers. She stops in front of us, running on the spot, then pulls a thin whistle out of her pocket and blows into it. I can't hear anything, but every dog instantly stands to attention. She jogs around in front of us, looking at each dog in turn, never once lifting her gaze to the humans. We could all be stood here dressed as clowns for all she knows. All the dogs are looking back at her. Except Gizmo. He's spotted a squirrel sitting on a gate and I can tell he wants a rumble. I silently will him to be a good boy.

The woman's eyes narrow, the whistle still clamped between her teeth. Then she whips it out.

'Sit!' It's so sudden, I actually cry out a little. As soon as she says it, every dog sits down. Every dog except one. Oh no.

'Roll over!'

Every dog rolls over in perfect synchronicity. Except one.

'Beg!'

Sure enough, they're all perfect. Again, except one.

She crouches in front of Gizmo and stares at him. He yawns and scratches behind his ear with his back leg.

'So who's this little man?'

Gizmo carries on scratching. She glances up at me, still not making direct eye contact. Ah, she wanted me to answer. Makes sense, really.

'Oh, uh, Gizmo.'

She carefully puts her hand on Gizmo's snout and lifts his top lip with the other. She runs her finger along until she has inspected everything.

'Fourteen,' she says.

'No, he's got way more teeth than that.'

I hear someone snigger behind me.

'I meant that's his age, my love.' She runs a finger along his spine.

'That's right,' I say.

Wow. She can tell a dog's age by looking at their teeth? She should go on *Britain's Got Talent*.

'I didn't see your name on my list,' she says, still not taking her eyes off Gizmo.

I take a breath. How am I going to get out of this one? 'Oh,' I say. 'We've definitely paid, you know, the three hundred pounds. Maybe Margaret didn't refresh the database.'

That wasn't bad. I threw in a couple of details that an intruder definitely couldn't have known. Not bad for off-the-cuff George. The last time I had to

quickly improv a lie was when Mr Brandrick wanted
to know why I was hiding behind the supplies
container during PE and I told him I had explosive
diarrhoea.

The woman nods. 'OK
then, I'm Sharon. I own
Practically Pawfect.' She still
hasn't looked at me properly. It's kind of weird. She
claps her hands. 'Sit.'

Gizmo does not sit. In fact, he seems to stand up
even taller.

'Sit.'

Gizmo jumps up and kisses her on the face.

Sharon laughs. 'Looks like I have my work cut
out here. Tell you what—I'll let you have a free trial
lesson. I like a challenge.'

She stands up and flashes a dazzling white grin at
me. 'I know you haven't paid, my love.'

I try to protest but my mouth flaps like a flag in a
gale.

'It's OK. Like I say, consider this a free trial.'

Sharon claps and addresses the other dogs. 'OK
my little furry adventurers, today we will be doing
the assault course. Follow me.'

We follow her through an archway which leads

to a field. Man, it really is an assault course. There's massive truck tyres, a see-saw, cones, all kinds of stuff. Gizmo starts pulling on the lead and I have to hold him back. He loves things like this.

'Um, excuse me?' Zirconia's owner puts her hand up like she's asking permission to go for a wee. 'That looks awfully muddy.'

Sharon nods. 'We've had a little rain recently.'

'But I've just had Zirconia groomed.'

'It's nothing a bit of shampoo won't fix,' says Sharon.

The other owners glance at each other nervously. 'Yeah,' says Zirconia's owner, 'but I think we'll sit this one out all the same.'

'We will too,' says the Corgi's owner. 'Getting dirt out of Eugenie's fur is a dreadfully arduous task.'

All the other owners stare at the floor. It's like when a teacher asks a hard question in class and everyone prays they're not going to get picked on.

'Gizmo,' she says. 'Do you fancy a go?'

She unclasps Gizmo's lead and touches his head, and without any more prompting, he takes off across the field, sprinting up and down the see-saw, between the cones and through the tyres. When he gets to the end, he goes back to the beginning and does it all over again. He's having the time of his life. I whoop and cheer as he makes his way back. You wouldn't know he's fourteen. He's like a pup again.

He trots right back to the middle of the circle and looks at all the other dogs like, 'What's the big deal?' I've never felt prouder of him. Way to show them who's boss! But wait. He's muddy. Really muddy. This isn't going to end well.

Gizmo shakes himself so violently, everyone within a three-mile radius gets spattered.

'Argh, my Louis Vuitton!'

I try my best to apologize and not laugh my absolute bum off, but it's a real struggle. Zirconia's owner glares at me like she wants to wrap Gizmo's lead around my neck and swing me around her head. None of the other owners seem too pleased, either. I try and put Gizmo's lead back on, but he whizzes around in a circle chasing his tail before dropping into the mud and rolling around.

None of the other dogs go on the assault course so it's back to the patio for more command practice. Sharon keeps trying to get Gizmo to sit, but he won't do it. In the end, she has to force his bum down and feed him loads of treats.

'I don't normally do it this way, but needs must,' says Sharon, before standing Gizmo back up. 'Gizmo, sit!' This time he does it. I can't believe it—Gizmo has actually done a trick! Admittedly, it's the easiest trick in the world, but at least it's a start.

Sharon goes back to the other dogs and I give Gizmo a fuss. He wags his tail super hard in that 'YES, I'M A VERY GOOD BOY' way of his and gives me a kiss.

After a while, Sharon says, 'OK, my little love creatures, excellent work. I'll see you next time.' She claps and beams at all the dogs, before fixing her gaze on me. 'I'll see you out, young man.' The grin never leaves her face. It's kind of unsettling.

She walks us across the patio to the gate.

'So,' she says. 'Did you enjoy that?'

I nod so enthusiastically, my head's in danger of flying off my neck.

'Good. But if you want another lesson, you'll have to pay.'

'OK,' I say. 'I'm, uh, a bit short of cash at the moment.'

Sharon's smile tightens. 'How much do you have?'

I rummage in my pockets. 'I've got . . . three . . .

sixty. I can probably scrape ten with my savings at home.'

Sharon is still smiling. Can she stop? Is she stuck like that?

'I'm afraid that won't be enough.'

I take a breath. Maybe if I tell her about the bucket list and the dog show, she'll take pity on me and at least give me a few pointers about how to train Gizmo. I try it. It doesn't work.

'I'm not running a charity, my love,' she says. 'Besides, if I give you my techniques, you might go off and start your own dog-training company.'

'But I'm thirteen.'

Sharon scrunches up her nose. 'Be that as it may, I'm going to have to ask you to leave.'

The gate swings open and Sharon, still grinning like she's just won the lottery five weeks in a row, motions for us to leave.

I grumble to Gizmo as we head back up the path towards the shops. If I had three hundred quid, I wouldn't need to enter the dog show. We could just go straight to Golden Beach.

'Hey!'

We carry on walking.

'Hey, dog boy!'

I stop. Who's this now? I turn around and see a girl walking towards me. She looks kind of familiar, but I can't figure out where from. She's wearing a black beanie hat and purple overalls. She's tall, too. And big.

'Old Sharon wouldn't help you out, eh?' she says, standing in front of me with her arms folded.

I shake my head.

'Doesn't surprise me. You should try asking her for a day off.' She holds out a hand. 'Name's Lib.'

I reluctantly shake her hand. Man, she is strong. I think she might have crushed my knuckles into dust. 'George.'

'And who's this young gent?' She breaks the shake and kneels next to Gizmo. She scratches the bit behind his ear that makes his back leg go. How did she know that's his sweet spot?

'Gizmo,' I reply, rubbing my hand.

'Cool name,' says Lib, by now scratching Gizmo's belly because he's rolling around on his back. 'You wouldn't fit in here, mate. Today, I shampooed a French Bulldog called Leopold.'

I can't think of anything to say.

'So I overheard you talking about Gizmo's bucket list.' Lib says, standing up and towering over me again.

My cheeks burn. For some reason, I feel proper embarrassed about it.

'I think it's a really sweet idea. It's like the two of you are on a quest or something,' she says.

Why am I still blushing? Stop blushing, idiot. I suppose I've never thought about it that way, but maybe she's right. It kind of is a quest.

'I want to help you,' she says, breaking the silence.

'Really?'

'Really,' she says. 'It's nice to meet someone who truly loves their dog and isn't just using him to makes themselves look rich or glamorous. Besides, I'm trying to become a proper trainer and groomer but Miss Bossybum won't give me a chance to learn. Gizmo could be my little guinea pig.'

I glance down at Gizmo rubbing himself up a plant pot. She's going to have her work cut out for her.

'Come back here on Monday at four. I'll meet you by the gate. The boss will be away at a conference so it'll be fine,' she says.

'Um, OK,' I say. 'Thank you.'

Lib winks. 'No worries, mate. I think this is going to be a lot of fun.'

Chapter Ten

OK, here we go. My costume is ready. It took me ages to figure out what I was going to wear. See, Mum's not exactly keen on me spending money on a fancy dress outfit. And Dad? Forget about it. He's still narked off about having to shell out for Gizmo's antibiotics. So I had to improvise. I dragged an old fake-fur coat out of Mum's wardrobe and put it on. Maybe I could go as Cruella de Vil? Or button it up over my face and call myself Chewbacca? No, I looked stupid. Besides, that thing has been in there for years and probably has fleas.

I thought maybe I would just go in my regular clothes, but Matt kept telling me at school I had to be in fancy dress otherwise I wouldn't be allowed

in. Seems a bit strict for a party but what do I know?
I was rifling through my wardrobe and getting
more and more desperate when I saw it. Of course.
Right at the back under a pile of old shoes. My
Intergalactic Power
Squad box. I hadn't
had that out in ages.

I dragged it out
and opened it. Wow. It still looked good. The red
U insignia, the yellow cape. I didn't think it would
fit but it does. Kind of. As long as I don't attempt to
dance or run or stand up too fast, I should be fine.

Underneath my outfit was another one: Wonder
Dog's. I managed to get the costume on Gizmo: the
yellow cape that matched mine and the red top with
the blue W insignia. I put it on him and it fits a lot
better than mine. Must be this rank new diet Mum's
put him on. Speaking of which . . .

'George, Gizmo, dinner!' Mum calls up the
stairs. Gizmo's eyes go from merely excited to
OHMYGODTHISISTHEBESTTHINGEVER
in a millisecond. I grab him before he can get to the
stairs, and strip the costume off him. It's like trying
to dance with an angry octopus. I don't know what
he's so excited about, dinner's not going to be half a

tin of Meaty Munch and a Jammie Dodger. By the time I've changed back into my normal clothes and caught up with him in the kitchen, reality has hit home like an articulated lorry.

'Two words,' says Mum. 'Cauliflower. Steaks.'

'What's that?' I say as I sit at the table. 'Steaks shaped like cauliflower?'

Mum chuckles. 'In your dreams.'

She slides a plate in front of me. There's a stack of green beans, a pile of rice, and what looks like two sliced clouds.

'I got the recipe from Nigella,' Mum says, sitting opposite me.

I poke at the 'steaks' with my fork and wince. If I had Nigella's address I'd stick them in an envelope and send them back to her.

'Very healthy,' Mum goes on, chomping on a mouthful.

I glance at Gizmo in the corner and see him gingerly nibbling at the edges of his steak. He must be starving if he's actually eating that. I try a piece and am kind of annoyed that it's not too bad. I mean, it's not great, but it's not as disgusting as I was expecting.

'See?' says Mum, proving that she has mystical

mind-reading powers over me. 'Vegetables can be tasty.'

Maybe she's right. This might change my entire view of the world. I don't think I'm ready for such a life-altering event.

'Don't forget you're staying over at Dad's tonight,' Mum says. 'He'll pick you up from the party.' My heart sinks a little, which sucks because I don't know why. Maybe I shouldn't think about it too much. Don't want to have a freakout.

It doesn't help that I'm nervous about this party. School parties aren't really my thing. The last one I went to was Damien Collins's in Year Five and I had to leave that early because the ice cream gave me a headache.

What if Matt doesn't want to know me? I wanted to meet him on the way so we could go in together, but he said he'll be going straight from the dentist's and will meet me there. Going in alone is going to be scary. What if I say or do something wrong? I don't know what high school parties are like. The only ones I've seen are in films and they always have loud music and dancing and things called 'kegs'. Is it too late to find out what a keg is? I get so nervous

I lose my appetite and slip the rest of my cauliflower steaks to Gizmo, who seems to be loving them by now.

I head back upstairs, put the costume back on, and look at myself in the full-length mirror. I look stupid. They're going to laugh at me, and not in a good way. See, there's two kinds of laughter; and it's not as simple as laughing with someone and laughing at them. Sometimes laughing at someone is fun. I remember last summer when I drew a moustache and furry eyebrows on my face and pretended to be our old head teacher Mr Lyons, Matt laughed so much he nearly peed himself. That was fun. The other kind was a few weeks ago when Tyler got right in my face and went, 'HURPADURPDURP,' which made Matt laugh until he (again) nearly peed himself. That laughter is different. It's harder, with a sharper edge, like a barbed wire fence, designed to keep me out.

I shoot Matt a text.

We're going as Ultra Boy and Wonder Dog.

He replies straight away.

Wicked man. Can't wait to see you.

Wow. Suddenly, I'm not so nervous. He's not going to laugh at me. Besides, he's seen those costumes millions of times. Actually, this gives me an idea.

Hey, if it's not too late, why don't you wear your AntiMatter Kid costume? Be like old times.

I wouldn't have asked him before, but after he was so cool about me being Ultra Boy, maybe he'll be up for it.

He replies with three thumbs up emojis. I smile and close my phone. Gizmo sprints upstairs and paws my leg.

'What do you know, Wonder Dog?' I say, in the Ultra Boy voice I haven't done in ages. 'Looks like the Intergalactic Power Squad are having a reunion.'

INTERGALACTIC POWER SQUAD

You wouldn't know it to look at me, but I have saved entire galaxies. I might scratch a lot and chew my own bum, but without me, entire worlds would not exist.

The Intergalactic Power Squad is made up of Ultra Boy, Wonder Dog, and AntiMatter Kid. We travel across space in the Power Ship and defeat enemies like Chronotron the Time Ripper, and Monstroso the Evil Space Octopus.

Of course, you might say that these are only stories that George wrote, but when he reads them to me, they feel real. I sometimes fall asleep afterwards and dream about slaying space creatures.

When we were younger, the three of us used to play in the back garden, zooming across the muddy lawn like it was the stars over Jupiter. I'd run with them and jump and bark and have the best time.

Sometimes, when AntiMatter Kid wasn't around, we'd have adventures as a duo and George would write about them. The longest one was about

Wonder Dog saving Ultra Boy's life. George was so
into that one, he cried at the end.

Even though I'm roughly seventy-eight in dog
years, I'd love to have one more Intergalactic Power
Squad adventure.

Chapter Eleven

We turn onto the road Casey Marshall lives on. I get Mum to drop us off around the corner just in case anyone is outside. I can't imagine being seen in Mum's old Corsa will do me any favours. I walk quickly and begin to panic that I might go to the wrong house, but I can hear the music already. Kind of. It's just like *BANG BANG BANG BANG* at the moment but it keeps getting clearer. The reunion is going to be so great. I can't remember the last time the Intergalactic Power Squad did anything together. Maybe we'll have another adventure. Maybe this will be the best party ever. Even if it's not, we'll get to tick something off Gizmo's bucket list.

We walk up the drive. I catch a glimpse through

the window and see there's quite a few people there already. It's pretty dark so I can only see shapes and shadows, but it looks busy.

I try the door but it's locked. Weird. I give it a knock but no one can hear it over the music. I try again, louder this time, but then I notice a doorbell. That might do it. I press it and the music volume suddenly drops. I see a pair of eyes flash by the frosted glass in the door. Then hushed talking. I hear footsteps. What's going on?

The front door opens and everyone is there. Literally about thirty people crammed into the hallway. And they're all laughing at me. Properly *at* me. Barbed wire fence laughter. None of them are dressed up.

I see Casey somewhere in the middle, with Tyler and Ethan at the front. The world seems to go into slow motion. Fingers point at me like I'm some kind of freak. I see every popular kid in our year opposite me, roaring with laughter. And at the back, leaning against the wall and smirking, is Matt. Not in his AntiMatter Kid costume.

I glance down at Gizmo and he's scratching like he wants to get the costume off. Surely dogs don't feel embarrassment. They can't even blush, can they?

I turn to leave but Matt pushes through the crowd and grabs me.

'Come on, Georgie Boy,' he yells right into my ear. 'It's only a bit of fun.'

The crowd begins to disperse as we're pulled inside. The laughter is still there, but it's dissolving across the house. Why didn't I bring a change of clothes as a backup? Gizmo can go naked. I very much can't.

Casey stops on the way back to the lounge, clicks her fingers at me and says, 'Oi, Superman, this is a shoes-off house, yeah?'

I grumble as I try and kick off my trainers. They're on too tight so I sit down on the stairs and undo the laces. Man, this costume is snug. I see Matt's red trainers sitting apart from everyone else's by the door. I swear he likes those things more than his own mum.

The music starts blasting again and everyone gradually goes back to their conversations. I grab Matt by the elbow but he shakes me off.

'What was that all about?' I yell over the terrible music.

'What was what all about?' he says, his eyes fixed on some girls over by the window.

I grab his arm again and hold on tight. 'You totally

humiliated me.'

He shrugs. 'Wasn't my idea. Take it up with Ethan and Tyler.'

He nods at the two silverback gorillas who seem to be trying to figure out which of them can headbutt the wall hardest.

'But you knew about it?'

He shrugs again. 'I don't know. Why can't you be cool, anyway? Get a sense of humour.'

Yeah, I'm sure he'd have a sense of humour about it if it happened to him. Fact is, he knew what they had planned for me and did nothing about it.

'Another thing,' says a voice from behind me. I turn around and Casey's in my face again, sneering at me. Her face is permanently like that. She could find a million quid in her wardrobe and she'd still look like someone had puked on her chips. 'You can't have that dog in the living room.'

That dog? What a CHEEK!

'What?' I say, letting go of Matt. 'Why can't Gizmo stay in the lounge?'

Casey pulls a face like someone's waving a dirty nappy in her face.

'Cos he's dirty and his hairs will get stuck in the carpet,' she says.

I start to say, 'He is NOT dirty,' but I can't even finish the sentence before he's dragging his bum across the pile like he's trying to win first place in a bum dragging race.

'Get him out of here right now,' Casey screeches while everyone laughs.

I grumble under my breath. 'This is supposed to be a fancy party, Gizmo. Why do you have to show me up?' I bend over to pick him up but as soon as I grab him, I feel something go. Something's not right. There's a tearing sound even louder than the music. Oh no. I haven't farted, have I? No. This is much worse.

'Oh my days, I can see his pants!'

I snap upright like I'm spring-loaded and touch the affected area. Yep. Massive rip. Why did I have to wear my hot-pink Y-fronts? Why? Everyone crowds around me laughing for the second time in about three minutes. Ethan drifts a little too close to Gizmo and I feel him growling against my chest.

'What stupid knock-off superhero are you supposed to be, anyway?' Ethan snorts.

'I'm not a knock-off, I'm an original creation,' I say, desperately trying to close the gap in my trousers. 'I'm Ultra Boy and this is Wonder Dog. And Matt was supposed to be AntiMatter Kid.'

Tyler giggles and punches Matt's shoulder. 'You his little sidekick are you, Matty?'

Matt shoves him and readjusts his hair. 'I don't know what he's talking about.'

'Are you serious?' I cry out. 'We were the Intergalactic Power Squad!'

Everyone starts giggling and Matt turns the colour of his ridiculous trainers.

'Hey Casey,' he says. 'Shouldn't George be getting out of here with that dog?'

'Yes!' Casey screeches, on her way back from the kitchen with a bowl of hot soapy water. 'In the conservatory. Now!'

I run out to the conservatory, still carrying Gizmo. I think about just leaving but then my bum would be exposed to the elements. Better to stay put until Dad picks me up. In . . . I look at my phone . . . THREE HOURS? Ugh. No thanks. I go to text him then stop myself. It always takes him ages to answer those things. Better to give him a call. I slump in a wicker chair, which thankfully has a cushion on it.

'You OK, George?' he says.

'Fine,' I say, ruffling Gizmo's fur and trying not to look at Matt attempting to chat up Hannah Armitage in the living room. 'I was just wondering if you could pick me up earlier?'

The line goes quiet and I have to stick my finger in my ear because someone has cranked up the music. 'Can you hear me?' I yell.

'That might be a bit of a problem, Georgie.'

I close my eyes and sigh. 'Really?'

'Yeah, I'm, uh, kind of tied up at the moment. Working late, you know.'

I don't say anything. He's been tied up a lot lately. Like, most of the time. 'How long until you can get here?'

'About an hour,' he says.

I huff. 'Fine.'

'Everything is all right, isn't it?' he says. 'Not in trouble are you?'

I think about it. I could tell him I'm in someone's house with my bum out but decide not to. If he's tied up, he's tied up. I'll just have to make myself as comfortable as possible.

'No, I'm fine. See you later.'

I suppose I could try to have it out with Matt again. I need to find out what's happening with him. But I can't go in the living room with Gizmo and besides, I don't want to run back into that lion's den.

I need him to come to me. So I wait. And wait. Gizmo gets bored and falls asleep on the floor.

It must be over an hour before Matt comes close enough to the door for me to shout him over. He ducks his head out. 'What do you want?'

'I need to talk to you.'

He looks back into the house as if to check he isn't being watched then steps out into the conservatory. 'What?'

This is brilliant. Being treated like some annoying five-year-old.

'What do you mean "what"?' I snap. 'For the past few months you've done nothing but embarrass me.'

Matt smirks. 'You need to lighten up, mate.'

'No, I don't,' I say. 'You need to stop pretending to be something you're not.'

This time he laughs. Not a proper laugh, like he used to do, but this weird laugh him and his ManDem crew all do. It sounds like a goat with its goolies snagged on a gate.

'Says the kid in a superhero outfit,' he drawls.

I go to stand up but I don't want to make my rip bigger so I stay put. 'You should be in yours,' I hiss. 'You're supposed to be AntiMatter Kid.'

Matt leans on the door and stares at me like I've

just asked him to sprout wings and fly to Neptune. 'George, I threw that thing out ages ago.'

I gasp. Actually properly gasp like my nan did when my cousin Darcy accidentally swore during the nativity play. My face burns up, my mouth flaps open and shut. There's so much I want to say but it won't come out. How could he do that?

He leans closer to me and pats me on the shoulder. 'If you want my advice,' he says. 'You need to grow up a bit. Superheroes are for babies.'

I'm still trying to force some words out of my mouth but it's useless.

'Otherwise the only mate you're going to end up with is your dog,' he says, before winking at me and walking back into the living room.

I look at Gizmo. His paws are twitching. He must be dreaming. I remember once, he got so into a dream that he got up and ran into the wall in his sleep. I felt bad for laughing but it was hilarious. I lean down and stroke his snout. Maybe he's the only friend I need. He's never outgrown me. He'd never embarrass me for a cheap laugh. I stare at him until the rumblings of a freakout subside.

Everyone starts filing through the conservatory into the back garden, yelling something about, 'taking this party outside.' I don't know why they'd want to do that. Maybe they feel like they're not annoying enough people by containing their idiocy indoors. A few of them say stuff to me as they go by, but I ignore them. Matt pretends I'm not there and rides past on Tyler's back, both of them laughing that stupid goat laugh. Billy Parsons nearly trips over Gizmo and wakes him up. Gizmo is so startled he lets a fart go.

Except it isn't just a fart, it's a war crime. God, my eyes are watering.

'Wow, Gizmo,' I splutter, trying to waft it out the door. 'What's wrong with your insides?'

He jumps to his feet and looks up at me, his eyes big and his mouth open. I hear a noise that sounds like thunder coming from somewhere in his undercarriage. Oh no. This is bad. I've heard this sound a few times before. It means there's going to be an explosion. A poo explosion. In less than a minute it's going to come shooting out like the world's most disgusting volcano. I grab the door handle but then I stop. I can't let him go out there. For one thing, Casey will absolutely freak, and two, it'll just be another thing for them to make fun of me about.

The rumble comes again, this time louder. Oh no.

It must be all those cauliflower steaks. His system isn't used to that many vegetables. I quickly scoop him up and run through the lounge.

When we get into the hall, I put him down so I can slip my shoes back on but **PPRRRRRRRRRPPPP**. Gizmo spins around super quick then lets it go. Straight into one of Matt's immaculate red trainers.

'Whoops,' I say, throwing my own untouched shoes back on. 'We should probably get out of here.'

I guess I should feel bad about this. I don't, though. It's brilliant.

GO TO A PARTY ✓

Dad

I used to have a good relationship with Dad. He always walked me and played with me. He called George and me 'my two boys'.

But as I got older, he got more distant. Especially after the incident. After the incident, Mum and Dad argued a lot. I remember slamming doors and the car screeching away. I'd sit on the windowsill like Reginald until he came back. But one day, he didn't.

Chapter Twelve

We're sitting in a pub restaurant by the canal. We've had to leave Gizmo tied up outside because Dad says they don't allow dogs. I pointed out that we've taken Gizmo in there before, but he just muttered something about a change in management and rushed me in.

I'm propping my head up on my fist. God, I'm tired. I didn't sleep last night. Partly because the bed in Dad's spare room is about as comfortable as a sack of porcupines, and partly because I kept replaying the party over and over in my head. The only reason I was ever invited was for them to laugh at me. I was like a clown they'd hired, except I definitely didn't get paid. I switched my phone off last night and haven't dared to turn it back on. I can't help but wonder how Matt reacted when he found his trainers had been poop-bombed, though. I smirk to myself and stir the ice in my drink with a straw.

Dad drums his fingers on the wooden tabletop and cranes his neck so he can see the door. He told me we were here to talk about something important, but so far it's just been boring football chat, which he knows I'm not into. I wonder what we used to talk about before he left. Was it always this awkward? When I was born did he just shake my hand and nod? I can see Gizmo outside. I can tell he wants to go and harass some Canada geese but his lead is holding him back. Probably for the best. Those things are vicious.

Dad clears his throat and points at his glass. 'This beer, um, ale actually, was brewed in Belgium.'

'That's fascinating,' I say, despite the fact that it is the least fascinating thing anyone has ever said in the history of the world. 'How come you've got two drinks, anyway?' I nod at the glass of wine next to his beer.

Dad gulps and looks like he's trying to figure out what to say. Oh God, is he one of those alcoholics like you see on *EastEnders*? I can't picture Dad stashing secret bottles and working at a car lot, but who knows?

Suddenly he stands up and smiles. I turn around and there's a woman walking towards us. She's about Dad's age. Black hair. Loads of clickety-clack bracelets on her arm.

'George,' says Dad. 'This is my, um, friend, Rosa. Rosa, this is my son, George.'

Rosa sticks her hand out and smiles. 'Oh George, I've heard so much about you.' Her voice is all posh and whispery, like she's commentating a croquet tournament.

I ignore the hand and give her a quick thumbs up. Something about this whole situation is weirding me out. I wish Gizmo was in here. She sits down opposite me.

'Oh, thank you Carl,' she says, taking a sip of the drink.

'No problem,' says Dad. 'Hey, what's say we grab some lunch?'

'Hold on a second,' I say, cutting him off. 'Who are you?'

'George!' Dad snaps, but I ignore him. After last night, I'm not in the mood for this.

Rosa touches his arm and smiles at me. 'I'm

Rosa,' she says, really slow and as if I've just woken up from a fifty-year coma and the Prime Minister is an ant. 'I'm a friend of your dad's.'

I fold my arms and glare at them. Since when does he organize trips to the pub to introduce me to his friends? Besides, she's not like any of his other friends. They're usually big hairy blokes with names like Gavin and 'Smelly Pete'.

'Would you like to know some more about me?' she goes on. I nod.

'Well, I, um, live in Stoneydale. I like music. For my job, I'm a social worker.'

I gasp. 'Is that what this is about? You're putting me up for adoption?'

Dad and Rosa both laugh but nothing about this is funny.

'No, son,' says Dad, gripping his stupid Belgian drink with two hands. 'I just wanted to introduce the two of you, that's all. Rosa is a very good friend.'

I groan. 'Enough. I'm thirteen years old. I'm basically an adult. She's your girlfriend, isn't she?'

I notice Rosa's face go pink. Dad can't even look at me. 'I know this can't be easy for you, Georgie, but—'

I stand up. 'Whatever. I'm going to check on Gizmo.'

Gizmo jumps up and nearly wags his tail off when he sees me. I sit at the table next to him and undo his lead so he can hop up next to me. He tries a couple of times but can't quite make it so I give him a lift up. He's been lying down for a while, so his legs have probably gone to sleep.

I ruffle his fur and watch an old couple work the canal lock. I've always found locks weirdly interesting, even though it's pretty much like filling up a bath then letting the water back out. Their boat is called *Sweet Freedom*. Man, I wish me and Gizmo lived on a boat like that. I could just chug away from my problems and moor up in a town with no Matts or Tylers or Ethans or Rosas. Speaking of which . . .

'Hi George,' she says.

I pick at a loose thread on Gizmo's lead.

She sits at the next table over. 'Hope you don't mind me coming out?'

I shrug. 'Not like I can stop you.'

I watch *Sweet Freedom* rise as the water gushes into the lock. Gizmo kisses the back of my hand, then lies down on the bench.

'Sorry I can't come closer,' she says. 'I'm allergic to dogs.'

I nearly fall on the floor. 'How can you be allergic to dogs?'

'It's the fur,' she says, wrinkling her nose. 'It brings me out in a rash.'

So that's why Dad didn't want Gizmo in the pub. I still don't get how you can be allergic to dogs. She must be a witch or something.

'Look George, I know the breakdown of your parents' marriage is an incredibly tough thing to go through,' she says, but I stop listening. I don't want to hear any of her social worker talk. I can tell she's said this stuff a billion times before. I don't need any of this. I just want to make the most of the time I have left with Gizmo and work through his bucket list. When did life get so complicated?

I grab Gizmo's lead and head off down to the towpath. I hear Rosa calling after me but I ignore her. We stride past *Sweet Freedom* and I nod at the old lady steering it.

I walk faster and faster, but I can't outrun what's happening to me—the tears, the short, jerky breaths, the tornado in my brain that sends thoughts hurtling in all directions at three hundred miles per hour.

We keep walking—the path stretching out ahead as far as we can see. I crouch under low bridges while

Gizmo yips at ducks. Eventually, we have to stop because Gizmo is tired. I look around and all I can see are fields with tight rows of crops being watered by huge sprinklers.

When Dad and Rosa find me, my face is wet. It was my first freakout in three months.

George's Freakouts

I know George better than anyone in the world, so I know all about his freakouts. That's what he calls them. Some people don't know how to deal with them when they happen. Some people fan him, some try and make him breathe into a bag. Matt used to be good with them, but lately he just gets exasperated and tells George to stop embarrassing him. I know all he needs is to be given some space and for me to be there for him. I shouldn't toot my own horn but I know how to calm George down better than anyone.

When they first started happening, I was a little frightened, but I soon got used to them. His first one happened when he was ten, not long after the incident. We don't talk about the incident that much.

George sometimes goes ages without having a freakout, but whenever he has one, I'm ready to help.

Chapter Thirteen

'There you are.' Matt stomps over to me outside school. 'I've been trying to get hold of you all weekend.'

'Really?' I say. 'Is it because I left the party without saying goodbye?'

He looks at me like I've just been beamed down from the planet Moronium. 'No, you idiot, I've been trying to get hold of you because you let your stupid dog take a massive dump in my best trainers.'

I struggle to hold in a laugh. This is the happiest I've felt for a while. I should have turned my phone on and let him call me yesterday. It would have improved my lousy trip to the pub no end.

'How do you know it was Gizmo?' I say. 'It might have been Tyler or Ethan. I'm pretty sure they're not potty-trained.'

Matt growls and grabs me by the lapels. He reeks of dodgy aftershave. 'I put my foot straight in that thing at the end of the night. Can you imagine the mess? And the smell?'

The thing is, that's exactly what I'm imagining and now I'm laughing. I bet he had a hard time impressing Hannah Armitage with his poo-sock of doom on. Oh Gizmo, just when I think I can't love you more.

Bang! I'm on the floor and my bum really hurts. He shoved me. Hard.

'Do not laugh at me, George,' Matt yells, standing over me and pointing.

I look up at him, at his weird hair and tie he wears super short, and realize that this is it. There's no way we can be mates any more. If I'm being realistic, we haven't been proper friends for about a year. It's time to cut the cord.

I stand up, ignore the crowds that are urging us to fight, and walk away. As I leave, I get this weird feeling in my stomach and my head seems like, hollow. I feel light. It takes me a minute or so to realize what it is: it's freedom. I don't have to worry about being good enough for Matt any more. I don't have to watch what I say in case it's not cool. I mean, yeah, I now have no human friends whatsoever, who need humans anyway? I'm not a sidekick any more. I'm not a 'who's your weird mate?' any more. I'm me. I'm George.

Ah, who am I kidding? Having no friends sucks.

I have to stand on my own at break time. Do you have any idea how awkward that is? Just standing there and staring at a field like a farmer on the lookout for foxes. I haven't even seen Matt since our bust-up this morning. He's probably lurking in the toilet with the ManDem like three unflushable poos.

At lunch I wander the corridors. You're not really supposed to do that, but I manage to dodge any teachers. It's a hot day and everyone else is outside. Everyone with friends, anyway. Even the library is deserted and you'd normally find at least a handful of goths taking shelter in the shadows behind the shelves.

I go in and flick through a few books but I can't concentrate on any of them. There's too much stuff going on in my head. Maybe I should go back and say sorry to Matt? Yeah, being friends with him was rubbish, but it wasn't as bad as being alone. No. Stay strong. You will find new friends. Proper friends. That's when a poster pinned to the wall catches my eye.

WRITING CLUB

EVERY TUESDAY LUNCHTIME IN THE LIBRARY.

Huh. Now that might be all right. I could write some new Ultra Boy and Wonder Dog stories there. Plus, I could meet friends that I have things in common with. No way would Matt go to a writing club. The only artistic thing he's ever done is write 'the ManDem' in biro on his pencil case. He'll be GUTTED when he sees all my new mates. He'll probably be all like, 'Oh George, your new friends are so cool and arty. Can I be part of your crew?' And I'll say, 'No, get stuffed mate.' And he'll have to hang around outside the library and watch us write and swap interesting anecdotes. That's right Matt, you just made the worst mistake of your life.

The Intergalactic Power Squad Go to Golden Beach.

Golden Beach was the first holiday I'd ever been on. Before that, it was just the odd day out here and there, and when George and Mum and Dad went away, they'd leave me with Auntie Gloria who would try and make me get on with her cat. Not happening. Sorry.

So I was super excited for the holiday. George had been writing loads of Intergalactic Power Squad stories about it—we were going to battle Crab People, Sand Monsters, and Aqua Demons. He read the stories to me in the back of the car on the way there. I stuck my head out of the window, and as the wind blew through my lips and ears I felt like I was riding across the galaxy in the Power Ship for real.

The main thing I remember from that time was how happy everyone was. They laughed and smiled and sang songs. George's freakouts hadn't started yet. He was ten years old. I was eleven. That's roughly sixty-five in dog years.

We rolled into a town on a long road with brightly coloured shops on one side and golden sands and blue water on the other. I couldn't wait to get out and run.

'What do you think, Wonder Dog?' said George. 'Ready for another adventure?'

Chapter Fourteen

After school, we head over to Practically Pawfect. Lib is waiting for us by the gates in the same purple overalls and black hat she had on the other day.

'You made it,' she says. 'Come on in.'

She leads me across the patio and into one of the converted stables. I know she said Sharon is away at a conference, but I'm still nervous she'll come back early and find me. Inside, the room is empty except for a box full of dog toys.

'We won't be disturbed in here,' says Lib. 'Right, Mr Gizmo, let's be having you.'

I let Gizmo off his lead and he darts straight over

to the toy box.

'Gizmo,' Lib says, her voice sharp. He turns around and his eyes lock onto a treat in Lib's hand. 'Sit.'

Gizmo's bum hits the floor like it weighs a ton. 'Wow.'

'Wow's right,' says Lib. 'I've been reading this book about dog training, and I reckon it blows Sharon out of the water. Not that she'll ever hear it. She's got her way and that's that. Hey, let's try something else.'

Lib gets a small treat out of her pocket which draws Gizmo straight to her. She gets him to sit again, then she tells him to lie down, moving the treat to the floor. Gizmo does as he's told and she gives him the treat.

'Who says you can't teach an old dog new tricks?' says Lib. 'Not that I'm saying you're old, mate.'

She carries on, getting Gizmo to sit and lie down again, then moving onto shaking paws. He starts off slowly but gets quicker every time. Probably because he knows it gets him treats. After about an hour, he's a well-oiled trick-executing machine. Well, he can do sitting, lying down, and shaking paws anyway.

'So, do you think you'll be able to get him good enough to win the dog show?' I ask.

Lib chuckles. 'I'll try my best. It's good to know he can do the basics, though. We'll try some more complicated stuff next time. So what else is on that bucket list?'

I decide to just pull it out of my bag and show her. For some reason, I get really self-conscious when I talk about it. Lib goes down the list and raises an eyebrow.

'What's so good about Golden Beach?'

I shrug and try not to make eye contact. 'Just a place we both like, that's all.'

'Ah ha!' Lib grins and smacks the list with the back of her hand. 'We can tick one of these off right now. Come with me.'

She produces a key from her pocket, opens the door next to me, and leads us into the fanciest dog-grooming salon I've ever seen. When Gizmo was younger, we used to take him to the Pooch Parlour on the High Street, but after Mum and Dad got divorced, it was Mum shaving him with some shears she'd bought off eBay.

I let out a whistle which echoes off every pristine white surface. I can tell Gizmo is trying to follow scents but it's so clean he keeps losing them.

'Pretty posh, yeah?' says Lib. 'I swear, this is nicer than the place I get my hair cut.' She grabs a pair of latex gloves and squeezes them over her hands, then pats a shiny silver table. 'Let's have him up here then.'

I must look confused because Lib makes a 'duh' face and says, 'This is Gizmo's pampering session.'

Oh, of course. Now I feel silly. 'Oh great,' I say. 'So, are you a trained dog groomer?'

Lib grabs a brush and starts running it through Gizmo's fur. 'Well, I don't have certificates, if that's what you mean, but I've been shadowing old Petunia for ages and I pretty much know how to do the job better than her. Luckily, they're all done for the day, so we have the place to ourselves.'

She runs a hand along his back and gently stretches his tail. 'He's a handsome boy,' she says. 'How old is he?'

'Fourteen,' I say. 'Roughly seventy-eight in dog years.'

'So you're an OAP then, mate. I'll be gentle.'

'I should warn you—he hates baths,' I say.

Lib chuckles. 'We'll see.'

I watch as she carries Gizmo over to a tub by the

wall and shampoos him, massaging his fur. His eyes are half closed and his back leg kicks out, a sure sign he's loving it.

'Wow,' I whisper. She must have a magic touch.

Lib rinses Gizmo off, then applies a different shampoo. It smells kind of salty. 'This is seaweed shampoo,' she says. 'It's good for terrier fur—makes it less coarse.' She massages it into Gizmo's fur and he purrs like a cat. Maybe it reminds him of Golden Beach. He loved rolling in the seaweed there.

'Does Sharon know you're doing this?' I ask, nervously eyeing the door.

'Nooooo,' Lib laughs. 'She would flip her wig if she found out. Gizmo's getting the gold treatment here—very pricey.'

She rinses off the seaweed stuff and starts applying some kind of facial wash, which Gizmo tries to lick off. 'This'll have him looking ten dog years younger,' she says.

'So how long have you been working here?' I ask.

'About a year,' Lib replies. 'I've done a bit of everything; assisting in here, mucking out kennels, sweeping up. All the stuff no one else wants to do.'

Once all the face stuff is washed off, Lib rubs cleaning gel into Gizmo's teeth, which makes him grin like he's posing for a school photo. 'You know, I think the bucket list thing is really cool,' she says. 'You must really love Gizmo.'

I swallow hard as my brain screams 'DON'T CRY, IDIOT' at my tear ducts.

'Yeah, I do.'

I step away for a second and pretend to be really interested in a box of dog poo bags. I take a minute to sort myself out before going back. I watch Lib's hands work quickly on Gizmo, washing him and keeping him comfortable at the same time. She's brilliant at it.

'Do you have a dog?' I ask.

Her smile shrivels a little as she towel-dries Gizmo. 'No, I don't. It's just me and Mum.'

The way she says it makes it seem like she doesn't want to talk about it any more. I decide to let her get on with it for a while.

She moves speedily but gently, throwing in the occasional stroke and bit of fuss to keep him relaxed. She clips his claws and buffs them so they're so shiny you can see your reflection in them. By the time she's finished he looks like a new dog.

'Well, Mr Gizmo,' she says. 'If I do say so myself you look very handsome. You happy, George?'

I nod. 'Yeah. Brilliant.'

She makes a cocking sound and blasts me with a finger pistol. 'It's what I do.'

On the way home, I can't help but admire Lib's handiwork. Gizmo's fur glistens in the sunset, his teeth are cleaner than they've looked in years, he even seems livelier. He's pulling on the lead. I decide to make the most of it and go home through the park. I unhook the lead from his collar and watch as he takes off across the grass and runs down towards the lake. Oh no.

'Gizmo! No!'

I go after him but it's too late. He's in the water. He swims in circles, yipping with happiness. I should be horrified that he's ruining his makeover, but watching him have fun is better than anything in the world. And that's what I've made this bucket list for, after all—for Gizmo to be happy and have as much fun as possible before, well, you know. Ah well, smartness wouldn't suit him anyway.

GET PAMPERED ✓

My Beauty Regime

It takes a lot of effort to look this good. My beauty regime is as follows:

- 🐕 A bath. Even though I love swimming, I hate baths. The water is too clean and soapy and there are no ducks to start a ruckus with. I will do anything to avoid the bath, up to and including squeezing through the fence and hiding behind next door's shed. Once I'm in there (the bath, not the shed), either George or Mum rubs me down with some liquid they call shampoo, then rinses me off with the shower. The jets of water are incredibly annoying and I will try to bite them.

- 🐕 De-fleaing. Fleas are tiny creatures that treat my body like a theme park. I try and scratch at them, but I can never get all of them. This is where the humans come in. They use this other shampoo on me which smells like burnt meat and makes my skin tingle. Then, they go through my fur with a comb and drag the fleas out. Somehow though, they always end up finding their way back to me. I must be a lot of fun.

🐕 Clipping. These days, Mum trims my fur in the kitchen. She stands me on some newspaper and uses a buzzy razor. When she hits a kink, she grunts the kind of words George would get in trouble for saying.

🐕 Teeth. This involves one human holding me down and the other one going at my teeth with a brush. They say this would only take two minutes if I stayed still, but, like, I don't want to.

The girl, Lib, was very good to me in the posh place. George seemed surprised that I stayed still, but she just had the touch. 10/10. Would recommend to other dogs. Except Reginald.

Chapter Fifteen

OK. Time for my first Writing Club meeting. I'm standing outside, psyching myself up. I don't know why. It's just a group of people writing together. I can see the clock on the wall from here. I'm going to walk in there in five seconds. OK, ten seconds. Fifteen.

The door opens and a Year Nine girl stands there. 'Are you here for Writing Club?'

I scratch the back of my head even though it's not itchy. 'Um, I think so.'

What kind of thing is that to say? I'm such a weirdo.

'Rrrright,' she says. 'Well, if you want to join us, we start in a couple of minutes.'

She goes back inside so I follow. There are four

people sitting around the table. They're all older so I don't know any of their names. I take an empty seat and look around. No one acknowledges me. They're all busy setting up their stuff.

I pull a half-finished Ultra Boy and Wonder Dog story out of my folder.

'OK everyone,' says the girl who let me in. 'It seems like we have a new member today, so I'll introduce everyone: I'm Molly, and this is Mia, Kate, and Ryan.'

They all half-heartedly nod at me. Not exactly the warm welcome I was hoping for, but OK, I can work on it.

'And you are?' says Molly.

I shake my head quick, trying to remember basic social interactions. 'Oh yeah. Sorry. I'm, uh, George.'

'OK,' says Molly. 'Well today, we're going to be doing some historical writing. And you've joined us for a very special session because we have the chance to interrogate a real historical figure. Could Socrates please come out?'

A figure begins to emerge from around the back of some shelves. It's a Year Ten kid in a toga. Literally a toga.

'PFFFFFFFF.' A noise involuntarily spurts out

of my mouth. Everyone stinkeyes me. I'm sorry, but come on. Why a toga?

'This is Socrates,' says Molly. 'An Ancient Greek philosopher.'

I highly doubt Socrates mooched about in his mum's bed sheets, but it doesn't matter. I have to make the best of this. I'm a bit disappointed because I thought we'd get to work on our own stuff and see what everyone is up to, but it looks like we all have to do the same thing.

Socrates sits at the head of the table and looks at us, blank-faced. He's wearing a fake beard made of cotton wool balls and I have to stuff my fist in my mouth to stop myself losing it. I'm trying to make friends and I'm not going to do it by laughing at their beards.

'So, Socrates,' says a girl I think is called Kate. 'What is life like in Ancient Greece?' I smile at her to show my approval for such a great question but she looks at me like I'm outside her window singing opera in my pants.

While Socrates speaks, I sense a shape in the window of the library door. Ugh. It's Matt, Tyler, and Ethan. The glass is warped and twists them into three cackling demons. Before I can move, the door opens and they stride in.

'Who's this then?' Tyler yells, striding over to Socrates. 'Santa on laundry day?'

Matt and Ethan sit at the table opposite. Everyone is pretending they're not there.

'Having fun?' Ethan chuckles at me. I ignore him and jot down some interesting things about Socrates, even though my hands are shaking.

A ball of paper hits me in the face.

'Hey!' says Ryan. 'That was my work!'

'Whatever, nerdbreath,' says Ethan, making Matt laugh like it's the wittiest thing anyone in the history in the world has ever said.

Tyler is standing right next to Socrates, who stays perfectly still, hoping perhaps that Tyler has reptilian vision like a T-Rex.

'He's like one of them guards at Buckingham Palace,' he yells. 'Boo!' He waves his arms around, but Socrates doesn't move. 'Wow, he's really good.'

I glance over at the library desk, but Ms Carnforth is on lunch and the student librarians have no idea how to deal with this.

'Hey lads,' says Tyler, 'let's see if this wakes him up.' He takes a deep breath, then launches the loudest, most disgusting burp I've ever heard right into Socrates's face. The great philosopher wretches and runs away so fast, he almost leaves his toga behind.

'Hey,' Molly yells, 'that is unacceptable.'

Tyler chuckles and sits down next to her. 'Well go and write a poem about it.'

Molly gathers her stuff, stands up, and storms off. The rest of the group do the same. Fantastic—I join a club and close it within ten minutes. I go to leave too, but Ethan grabs my shoulders and pushes me back down.

'Why you in such a hurry?'

'What do you want?' I say.

They all laugh. 'We just want to join your gang, Georgie,' says Tyler. 'Ain't that right, lads?'

'Yeah,' says Matt. 'I'm proper jealous of your new mates. I want to dress up in a sheet as well.'

I stare down at the table and slide a piece of blank paper over to him. 'Fine,' I say. 'You want to write, be my guest.'

'All right,' says Matt. 'Here we go.'

I hear him scribbling something on the paper. I'm still staring at the table and gripping my pen so tight I'm in danger of breaking it.

Another ball of paper smacks me in the face.

'You going to look at Matt's drawing or what?' says Ethan. 'He'll be offended if you don't.'

I sigh. I'm going to have to look whether I like it or not. I flatten the paper out on the table. It's a stick drawing of me with stink lines coming off it. I'm wearing a top hat, and a dog—probably supposed to be Gizmo—is in a wedding dress. On the top of the page, it says 'Lonely George.' I screw it up again and try to throw it in the bin in the corner, but I'm shaking so much I miss, which of course, they think is the funniest thing in the world.

'What a harsh critic,' says Matt.

I try to ignore them, but they keep throwing bits of paper at me. I can feel the fires of a freakout rising in my chest and start breathing heavily to put them out. In … out … in … out. Remember what Dr Kaur told you: this will pass.

I visualize rain falling on flames and think about Gizmo at home. He's probably asleep on his bed in the kitchen, chasing cats in his dreams. I want to go home and see him.

I must have got lost in thought at some point because I'm only just starting to register a chant. It's steady and rhythmic, accompanied by fists on the table.

'FREAKSHOW, FREAKSHOW, FREAKSHOW.'

I make eye contact with Matt. How is it so easy for him to forget all our years of being mates? The time we went camping and did a midnight rain dance? That time I fell in a brook in the woods and he laughed so hard he weed himself? When my parents split up and he put his arm around me and told me it was going to be all right? Is all of that gone to him?

I pick up my pens and stuff them into my case. I'll never get to make new friends with them around. I might as well just give up.

'What you writing about?'

I hear a voice next to me. It sounds familiar. I turn around and there is Lib. This is the first time I've seen her without a hat. One side of her head is shaved and the other side is all curly and scrunched. She's in a school uniform but her tie is super short with threads picked out of it.

'Um, just a . . . Greek philosopher,' I say.

Ignoring the chants, she slides the paper away, revealing the half-finished Ultra Boy and Wonder Dog story underneath, complete with illustrations.

'Mate, this is well good,' she says. 'Is this Gizmo?'

I nod.

'You've got a real talent,' she says. 'Which is more than I can say for these LOSERS.'

The chanting stops. Then the laughing starts.

'Who's this, Georgie, your girlfriend?' says Matt. 'Bit big for you, ain't she?'

Before he can utter another word, Lib jumps out of her seat, slides across the table, grabs Matt's arm, wrenches it behind his back, and pushes his face into the table. He screams as she cranks up the tension. Even Tyler and Ethan look terrified.

'You got something you want to say to me, Chuckles?' Lib growls.

'No!' Matt shrieks. 'Help!'

Lib lets go of his arm and he gets up and runs off, Tyler and Ethan trailing behind him.

I can't believe what I've just seen. I want to give her a hug, but I feel like she might body slam me through the table.

'Um, thanks,' I say.

''S all right,' she sniffs, sitting back down next to me. 'I was reading around the corner and I thought I recognized your voice.' She balls her hand into a fist and cracks her knuckles. 'I can't stand bullies at the best of times, but when they're picking on someone nice it proper yanks my chain.'

Everyone else in the library is looking at us, but Lib doesn't seem to care. 'Right,' she says, grabbing a spare sheet of paper. 'How about you teach me how to draw Gizmo?' I smile as the fires in my belly finally go out and my breathing returns to normal. Looks like I have made a friend after all.

Chapter Sixteen

I remember Granddad used to watch this cartoon called *Popeye*. It's about a squinty old sailor who's always getting into fights. Whenever he needs a bit of help, he downs a can of spinach and is suddenly the toughest man in the world. Well, that's what we've got for dinner tonight. Spinach. And I definitely don't feel tough. I feel sick, if anything. Gizmo has some sprinkled on top of his dry food mix and it looks like he's trying to eat around it.

Mum puts down her knife and fork and claps her hands together with her elbows on the table. Uh-oh. That's her 'we need a serious talk' stance. I can see it a mile off. I don't need this. I was in a pretty good mood, until now. The three idiots have been leaving me alone at school since Lib nearly ripped Matt's arm off.

'So,' says Mum. 'I was in your room earlier.'

I stop eating, which is kind of a relief, because it's horrible. 'Yes?'

Mum nods. 'I saw the bucket list.'

'What?' I yell. 'Who gave you the right to go through my private stuff?'

Mum gives me one of her trademark 'take it down a notch' looks. 'You left it lying on your desk and it caught my eye.'

I slump back in my chair. 'And?'

'And I think it's a really nice idea. But . . .'

Here we go.

'Why do you want to go back to Golden Beach?'

I shrug and stare at the green mush on my plate. 'Gizmo liked it there, that's all.'

'Yeah but, after what happened . . .'

'It's fine,' I say. 'I don't care about that.'

Of course, I do care, but I'm not going to talk to Mum about it.

'All right,' says Mum, holding up her hands. 'Well, as you know, money's a little tight at the moment, so we'll have to see.'

I'm not going to tell her about my dog show plan

because the idea of Gizmo winning anything to do with obedience would be enough to make her choke on her spinach.

'But I've spoken to your dad.'

OH GOD.

'Why would you do that?' I whisper, my throat too contorted with rage to even shout.

'Well, I saw you had camping on there and I thought that might be a nice thing for you to do together.'

I bury my head in my hands. They've been talking about me, I know it. Probably arguing.

'You know about that Rosa, right?' I mumble.

'Yes,' says Mum.

'Is she going to be there?'

'I don't know.'

Gizmo starts skittering around by the door so I get up and let him out. He goes straight to his usual weeing spot, the barbeque.

'Aren't you bothered?' I ask her.

Mum grasps her tea mug in both hands as if she really does wish it was Prosecco.

'Your father is free to see who he likes,' she says. 'Anyway, he said he'll pick you up tomorrow afternoon.'

I grip the door handle. 'Tomorrow afternoon? That might be a problem.'

'Why?'

I've arranged with Lib to meet up after school at Practically Pawfect to do some training with Gizmo.  She says the obedience school and salon close a bit earlier on a Friday, so we won't get hassled by Sharon. Thing is, I don't really want to tell Mum about it. Not yet. She'll ask loads of questions and, ugh, I just don't have the energy.

'I've, uh, got an after-school club.'

Mum raises an eyebrow. 'Since when do you go to after-school clubs?'

Damn. She's got me, there.

'Um, it's a new thing,' I say, trying to swallow the guilty feeling I get when I lie to Mum. 'Dog Club. That's why I've got to take Gizmo with me.'

Mum rolls her eyes and smiles. 'Dog Club, eh? Whatever next?'

'Yeah,' I say. 'Well, tell Dad to pick me up from school after six.' Practically Pawfect is only five minutes away so we should have enough time to get some work done.

Mum salutes sarcastically. 'Aye aye, Captain.'

Gizmo toddles back into the house and looks up at me. He knows something's up, I can tell. 'Well boy,' I say, 'looks like we're going camping with Dad.'

Gizmo stops for a second as if he's thinking about it, then turns around and runs to the bottom of the garden.

Why didn't I think of that?

The Holiday Park

I was so excited to see the Golden Beach Holiday Park. There was a lake, a huge field, and a massive assault course. I stuck my head out of the window and took it all in.

The house we were staying in was nothing like our usual one. There were no stairs or gardens. Mum and Dad called it a 'chalet'. I grabbed Mr Monkey and went off to explore. There were so many new smells, I didn't know where to start.

We found out that George and I had our own room and I even had my own bed. A human bed! I jumped up there and fluffed up the pillows and duvet until they were to my satisfaction. It was so comfy, I went straight to sleep.

If this is what holidays are like, I want them all the time!

Chapter Seventeen

When we get to Practically Pawfect, Lib is sitting on the wall, polishing off a pasty.

'Just finishing my dinner,' she says, brushing crumbs off her lap. 'Hope you appreciate me spending a rare afternoon off with you two.'

'Oh, so you're not working tonight?'

Lib shakes her head. 'I work after school four afternoons a week on a rota, though.'

'Four afternoons?' I say. 'That's a lot.'

Lib jumps down off the wall. 'Yep. Need the money, mate.'

'Are you saving up for something?'

'Something like that. Right, let's get going, shall we?'

We make our way through the gate, across the patio, and into the room where Lib gave Gizmo his first obedience lesson.

'By the way,' I say, 'I just wanted to say thanks for the, um, library thing.'

Lib laughs and lightly taps my cheek. 'I'll send you the bill for my bodyguard services at the end of the month. OK,' she clicks at Gizmo. 'Sit.'

Gizmo does it first time. Lib touches his neck then the ground. 'Lie down.' Gizmo does it. Lib touches Gizmo's nose. 'Roll over.' This time, he just cocks his head like, 'What?' Lib takes a treat out of her pocket, then, still holding it up, she gets down on the floor and rolls over.

'That's how you do it! Now you try.'

Lib guides Gizmo onto his side, then his back, then all the way around to a lying down position. He goes to take the treat, but she pulls it back. 'No, you can only have it when you roll over by yourself.'

Gizmo looks at me like, 'Is she serious?' then slowly rolls over. I fall to my knees and fuss him. 'That's amazing!'

'OK, OK,' Lib gives Gizmo a treat and gently guides me away. 'Well done, boy. You did good, but let's not get carried away.'

'I can't believe it,' I say. 'You're way better than Sharon.'

Lib blows a raspberry. 'It's not as hard as she makes it look. You have a go.'

'At what?'

'Getting him to do tricks. You're the one who's going to be doing the show.'

I climb to my feet and clear my throat. 'Gizmo, sit.'

Gizmo stares at me like I'm trying to explain how gravity works.

'Gizmo, sit.'

Gizmo turns around and chews on his tail.

'What am I doing wrong?' I ask Lib.

'You don't have enough confidence,' she replies.

'What do you mean?'

'I mean you give Gizmo orders with all the authority of a week-old lettuce,' she says. 'You need to show him who's boss.'

As soon as she says it, a montage of all the times Gizmo has demonstrated that I very much am not the boss whizzes through my mind.

Lib grabs my shoulders and pulls them back, then tilts my chin upwards. 'There, I just sorted your posture. You walk around like you're carrying the world on your back. Try standing up like you're not the missing link.'

Now she mentions it, standing up straight does feel kind of strange. I bet I've been walking around like this since I started high school. Like if I crouch and keep my head down, no one will notice me.

'Now try it again. With confidence.'

I take a deep breath and try and force some authority into my voice. 'GIZMO. SIT.'

Lib splutters with laughter. 'I'm sorry, George. I didn't mean to laugh, but when I said "with confidence", I didn't mean "like a dalek".'

I laugh a little. Why do I have no control over my own voice?

'Sorry,' I say. 'You must think I'm a weirdo.'

'Yeah,' says Lib, gripping my shoulder. 'That's why I like you.'

I blush as she gets Gizmo to beg in exchange for a treat.

'Besides, I'm used to weird people,' she says. 'There's loads of them in my block.'

Block? Like block of flats? So she doesn't live in a house. 'Oh. Whereabouts do you live?'

'Ampleforth Drive,' she says.

Ah. I had no idea. Everyone in town knows

Ampleforth Drive. It's the type of place you never walk on your own. Whenever something bad happens, you can guarantee an Ampleforth Drive resident was involved in some way.

'Yeah, I know,' she says, as if she can read my mind. 'Anyway, the guy that lives below us legally changed his name to "The Emperor".'

I laugh. 'That's brilliant!'

'I know, right?' says Lib, directing Gizmo to spin in a circle before offering him a little treat. 'You wouldn't expect royalty in that part of town, would you? And that's not the worst of it—he's kept his old name, too, so his legal name, on his ID and everything, is "The Emperor Colin Smith".'

This makes me laugh. Properly laugh. Like I haven't since . . . I can't remember the last time I laughed like that.

We try again and again to get Gizmo to obey my commands but nothing works. He does everything for Lib, though. She could probably get him to rob a bank or something. The show is just over a week away. I need to figure out how to be confident. Should be easy, right?

'Well, there's clearly no problem training Gizmo,' says Lib. 'Looks like it's you I need to work on. We'll sort out a day next week when you can come back. We close at six, so it'll have to be after then. I'll text you.'

'Sounds good,' I say. I get my phone out to put her number in when a message flashes up from Dad. It's a load of tent emojis and 'be there in five'. Great.

Camping

I've only been camping once before and that was in the back garden, just me, George, and Matt. This was before Matt became more bothered about his trainers than doing fun stuff.

Matt brought his tent around. It was just big enough for the three of us, plus Mr Monkey. They played computer games on their tablets, told ghost stories, and ate loads of snacks. Oh, I loved the snacks. Onion rings, Frazzles, popcorn. I was in heaven.

When it was getting late and the big humans had gone to bed, Matt had the idea of doing a rain dance. I didn't really understand why, because rain stops me going on walks, but I was happy to join in as they skipped around the tent and did silly chants. I got a bit too excited and started trying to join in with the chants myself, which made Dad come down and tell us to go to bed.

After that, they lay in the dark and laughed and talked nearly all night. Hey, even the Intergalactic Power Squad is allowed to be silly every now and then.

Chapter Eighteen

'This is the life, isn't it, son?' Dad winks at me, the campfire sending orange shards of light dancing across his face.

I mumble a bit and pass Gizmo a piece of my burger. His eyes light up like it's the greatest day of his life.

'I have found in my work that getting outdoors can have tremendous benefits to mental health,' says Rosa.

Ugh. Homeless people are in the outdoors but I doubt their mental health is brilliant. What a load of rubbish. Why is she even here anyway? I thought her dog allergy would keep her away, but apparently, she got some pills that treat the symptoms. Lousy medical breakthroughs.

Anyway, when I put camping on Gizmo's list, I meant somewhere fun where we could have adventures. Not in some random field in the middle of nowhere. There's literally nothing here.

'Would have been nice to have gone somewhere a bit, um, fancier,' says Dad. 'But, as you know...'

'Money's tight,' I say, finishing his sentence for him and trying not to eyeball Rosa's posh car parked nearby.

Gizmo nudges my leg for another piece of burger and I give it to him. He's been eating pickled cabbages or whatever for so long, he must be desperate for some meat. After all, he is descended from wolves, and you wouldn't catch a wolf eating that stuff.

'So,' says Dad. 'Who's up for a game of Travel Cluedo?'

'I would,' I say, standing up. 'But it's time for Gizmo's walk.'

Gizmo shoots me a look which is a mixture of 'Yay, walkies' and 'Why are we leaving the burgers?'

'Great,' says Dad, clapping and rubbing his hands together. 'We'll come with you.'

I grab Gizmo's lead and clip it to his collar. 'Yeah, it's actually more of a me and Gizmo thing. Besides, you shouldn't leave a campfire unattended.'

Dad puffs out his cheeks and nods. 'OK, but don't be gone too long.'

As I walk away I hear Rosa chuntering on about how it's important for Dad to give me 'space to breathe' and blah, blah, blah. I don't care. I just need to get away for a while. The last thing I need is for Rosa to lecture me about how playing Cluedo is good for your liver or whatever.

The sun is going down behind the hills in the distance. I check my pocket to make sure I have my torch with me. I remember Dad teaching me how to signal for help with it. Dot dot dot, dash dash dash, dot dot dot. Not that it would be any use. Anyone going past would just think I'm some idiot flashing a torch. We stumble over the bumpy ground, through long grass and mud patches, and take a little detour around a load of stingers before I let Gizmo off. I remember the time he cartwheeled into a patch of those and ended up with a face like lumpy custard.

When I unclip his lead, he takes off over the field and I have to jog to catch up with him. That vet doesn't know what she's talking about—he's not old at all. He's just as fast as he ever was. He stops under a tree then comes tearing back carrying a stick. He drops it at my feet and looks up at me, his tongue hanging out of the side of his mouth. I pick it up and launch it as far as I can. Gizmo disappears after it, leaping over a brook as he goes. I love watching him run. He looks so happy. Like he's never worried in his life. And I bet he hasn't. He doesn't have to think about school, and idiots like Matt, and his parents getting divorced, and his dad going out with some social worker who clacks when she walks. Just pure contentment.

I know dogs don't get to live as long as humans, but they have great lives while they're here. Well,

most of them do, anyway. I sometimes wonder
what would have happened to Gizmo if Mum and
Dad hadn't picked him at the rescue centre. Would
another family have taken him? What if they hadn't?
I shudder and wrap my arms around myself. It's
true that Gizmo was lucky we gave him a home, but
nowhere near as lucky as we are to have him.

And . . . and now he's rolling around in fox poo.
Great.

GO CAMPING ✓

Chapter Nineteen

We didn't rain dance around the tent last night.
We didn't need to. It absolutely lashed it down all
night. The only good thing about it is that it washed
Gizmo down. The bad thing was when he shook
himself all over the inside of the tent.

Today, we're on a 'nature walk' (Rosa's idea).
We've trekked for hours through woods and fields.
Rosa told us the names of all the trees and Dad was
all, 'Yeah, that's so illuminating.' This from a man
who only reads books about old footballers and
'East End hardmen'.

We've stopped for a picnic at the ruins of an
ancient priory. Rosa told us it was a 'fascinating site
of historical interest,' but it just looks like a pile of

graffitied stones to me. Imagine busting your hump building a place for a load of nuns to live, only for some spud-faced moron to write their gang name on it eight hundred years later.

'Puts things into perspective, doesn't it?' says Rosa. 'How the things we create in life live on long after we're gone.'

'That's really illuminating, Rosa,' says Dad.

Someone needs a thesaurus for Christmas.

'Actually, son, I've been meaning to talk to you about something,' says Dad.

I raise my eyebrows at him and feed Gizmo half a Scotch egg.

'Your mum told me about you wanting to go to Golden Beach.'

My stomach drops. As bad as it sounds, when I imagined going back there, I didn't picture Dad. Just me and Gizmo. And Mum I suppose. I nod.

Dad stares at the picnic table and twists the ring on his thumb. 'Why do you want to go back there? Of all places.'

I scratch behind Gizmo's ear. 'I just want Gizmo to play on the beach again, that's all.'

'There's plenty of beaches in the world, George,' says Dad. 'Why that one?'

Rosa puts down her juice carton. Here we go. 'Forgive me for interrupting, but this seems like a perfectly reasonable request from George.'

Dad's mouth tightens and he blinks hard. 'You don't understand, Rosa.'

'Well, I'd like to,' she says. 'Let's talk about it.'

'No,' Dad snaps. 'Forget I ever mentioned it.' And with that, he gets up and walks towards the ruins.

Rosa will learn eventually. We don't talk about Golden Beach.

The Sea

The holiday park was loads of fun. Once we'd unpacked, we went straight to the assault course. This was my favourite thing. I climbed up the ramps, hopped in and out of tyres, and slid down the slides on my belly.

George, Mum, and Dad watched me, laughing. Mum and Dad were different on holiday. They were relaxed. They smiled easier. More importantly, they bought me ice creams.

By the end of the first day, I was so tired that me and Mr Monkey fell asleep immediately. We were having the best time, and it was only going to get better.

The next day, we went out exploring the town. I decided Mr Monkey had to come and see the sights too, so I carried him around. Everywhere we went, I made people smile.

'Aww, look at him, he's got his little friend.' People even took photos of us, like we were a seaside attraction. It was quite nice to be the centre of attention. Back home, people were used to seeing us so we weren't a big deal.

If the holiday park had loads of smells, this place was ridiculous. There was fish and chips, the salty sea air, toffee. Dad bought me a saveloy and I gobbled it greedily under a big umbrella.

After we'd walked along the seafront, we crossed the road and went down the steps onto the beach. I'd never been on a beach before and I was freaked out by the way the sand shifted under my paws. It took me a while to get used to it, but soon I was running down to the water. Even that was different. It moved and pulled and sucked. I left Mr Monkey with Mum and Dad and found a stick some other dog had left. I dropped it at George's feet and wagged my tail. He knew exactly what to do, and I went sprinting into the surf, bobbing under for a second to get the stick before swimming back with it, the waves pushing me along. It was a magical feeling.

Chapter Twenty

With the camping trip of the century behind us, Gizmo and I head to Practically Pawfect for another training session with Lib.

She texted me earlier to sort a time when she was sure we wouldn't be disturbed.

Gizmo is already a little out of breath by the time we get there. He spotted a squirrel in the park and sprinted after it so fast he yanked the lead out of my hand. As always, the squirrel got away and scrambled up a tree, leaving Gizmo yipping up at it.

Things have changed since Gizmo's last trip to the vet. Before, when things like that would happen, I'd just laugh and be happy. Now, the happiness has a sad tinge to it—like a rumble of thunder in the distance on a sunny day. It makes me appreciate the sun more, but I can never truly ignore the storm clouds.

'Sorry I'm late.' I turn around and Lib is hurrying up to us, out of breath and red-faced.

'That's OK,' I say. 'Are you all right?'

'Fine,' she says, 'just Mum stuff.'

I don't really know what she means by that, but it doesn't look like she wants to talk about it. 'Anyway, I've been reading up more about advanced dog training methods and I want to try some of them out on Gizmo.' She uses her keys to let us through the gate and into the converted stable next to the salon. Everything is quiet and the lights in the main office are all off.

'The obedience school and the salon are closed now so we should be alright in here,' says Lib.

She sticks two fingers in her mouth and does one of those whistles adults seem to be able to do. Gizmo bounces over to her, sticking kisses all over her hands. She lets him for a few seconds then firmly says, 'Heel!'

Gizmo stops kissing and looks up at her, awaiting further instructions.

'Sit!'

Gizmo does as he's told.

Lib carries on with the lying down and rolling over he's already learnt. Next, she gets him to hold up his left paw, then encourages him to lift his right one at the same time. She slowly backs away, so he's left holding both paws up. 'Beg!' she says. Gizmo waves his paws in the air for a second before putting them back down. Lib fusses him and gives him a treat.

'Good boy! Now we're going to try something different. Something that will definitely win you that dog show if we can pull it off.'

The door rattles. Lib straightens up, her eyes wide. I hear what sounds like keys jangling. Lib scoops up Gizmo and puts him in my arms, then throws open the door that leads to the salon and shoves us through just as the main door opens.

'Lib? What are you doing here? We're closed.'

The sound is muffled but I can tell it's Sharon.

'Just hanging around. What are you doing here?' says Lib.

It goes quiet. So quiet, I'm beginning to panic that she'll hear Gizmo sniffing.

'It's my business and I can come and go as I

please, young lady. Now tell me why you're here.'

'Left some school stuff,' says Lib.

'In here?' Sharon asks, like she doesn't believe her.

'Yep. I come in here for my breaks and do homework. Always grinding, you know me, Shazza.'

'What have I told you about calling me that? Anyway, hurry up and clear out, I'm having some potential new clients around for a tour and I don't want you cluttering up the place.'

Huh. Sharon's kind of mean.

'Will do,' says Lib. 'Wouldn't want to upset the lords and ladies. I'll go out through the salon, yeah?'

'However you like, just do it quick,' says Sharon.

Wait, she's heading our way. I skip as lightly as I can and hide behind a wall. I hear Lib enter. 'George?' she whispers. 'You there?'

I stick my head out. Lib sees and points at the other door. 'We need to go.'

I follow her as she opens it and looks out. 'I don't know where she went,' says Lib. It's all quiet and I feel like Sharon could leap out at any moment like a tracksuit-wearing zombie.

'After three, we go,' Lib says. 'One . . . two . . . three.'

Lib pushes off through the door and runs for the gate. I follow behind, Gizmo bouncing in my arms. We don't stop until we're the other side of the shops.

Lib laughs. 'That was a bit close.'

'Too close!' I squeak.

Lib fusses Gizmo then clamps a hand on my shoulder. 'Looks like we're going to have to find a new place for training.'

Chapter Twenty-One

OK, so now we're in my back garden. We were going to go to the park, but Lib saw some girls from her year hanging around and decided she didn't want to deal with them when she's busy. I wasn't too crazy about the idea of coming back here, what with Mum being the most embarrassing person on Earth, but Lib is very persuasive.

'So where were we?' she says. 'Oh yeah, the game-changing trick. Gizmo, beg!'

Gizmo goes up on his back legs like he did before and Lib holds his front paws. 'Gizmo, dance,' she says, and slowly spins around with him. He lets her do it, too. Whenever I've tried to dance with him, he's gnawed at my hands like they were made of meat. Which they kind of are, I suppose.

Lib lets go and Gizmo's front paws land on the ground. She gives the order again but he just looks at her, so she gets him to beg and twirls him one more time, before giving him a little treat out of her pocket.

'OK, you should know what you're doing now,' Lib says. 'Gizmo . . . dance.'

Gizmo cocks his head and lifts a paw as if to say, 'Will that do?'

Lib plants her hands on her hips and sniggers. 'All right, boy. Time to break out the big guns.' She goes into her bag and pulls out a huge piece of burger wrapped in a serviette. 'I "borrowed" it from school.'

Now *that's* got his attention.

'Gizmo, dance!'

I can see something change in Gizmo's eyes. Like he's concentrating really hard. He slowly rises up on his back legs, and spins around.

'Oh my God!' I yell way too loud. Lib claps and whoops, a big proud grin on her face.

'Don't mind me, just passing by with refresh— WHAT'S HAPPENED TO THE DOG? IS HE POSSESSED?'

I spin around and Mum is there holding a tray that might as well be propping up her jaw.

'Lib's taught him some tricks,' I say. 'Pretty cool, isn't it?'

Mum places the tray down carefully, then fusses Gizmo who has finished dancing and is ready to feast on that burger. 'I never thought I'd see the day,' she says. 'Please, help yourselves.'

There's a couple of glasses of squash and some cookies on the tray. Wow. I can't remember the last time we had cookies in the house. It must be a special occasion.

'Oh, thanks, Ms Duggan,' says Lib.

Mum smiles unconvincingly. 'Please, call me Julie. So you're ... friends from school?'

I could tell she was looking at Lib and thinking she looks way too old to be my friend, but was too polite to say it.

Lib nods. 'Yeah. I'm a bit of a dog person so I'm helping George out with his list.'

'Oh, that's lovely,' Mum says, that fixed smile never leaving her face. 'Well, please do dig in. I made these myself.'

Lib and I take a cookie each. Since when does Mum bake cookies? Since when does she cook anything these days that isn't disgustingly healthy? I pick one up and take a bite and, oh.

'They're skinny cookies,' she says. 'The healthiest you can possibly eat!'

I exchange a quick look with Lib. This might be the worst thing I have ever put in my mouth. It has the texture of soggy cardboard and the taste of . . . soggy cardboard.

'Oh, these are delicious, Julie,' says Lib. 'I could eat a million of them.'

Is she being sarcastic? It's so hard to tell.

'You're too kind,' says Mum. 'They're so good for you, even Gizmo is allowed one!'

Thank God for that. I take one and pass it to him. He bites off a piece but immediately spits it out and coughs like he's been poisoned. Lib gives him a piece of the burger to take the edge off.

'Oh dear,' says Mum. 'All the more for you, then! If you need me, you know where I am!' I watch as she goes back into the house and sits at the kitchen counter, eyeballing us through the window.

'Sorry about her,' I say to Lib. 'She's so embarrassing.'

Lib takes a big gulp of squash and wipes her chin. 'Nah, she's cool. You're lucky to have her.'

I chuckle and stroke Gizmo as he comes back to sniff at his chewed-and-spat-out health biscuit. 'I don't know about that.'

Lib looks dead serious, her eyes wide. 'I'm not kidding. My mum never makes me cookies.'

I don't know what to say. I even consider eating the rest of my cookie for something to do.

Lib puts her glass back on the tray. 'Right, the show's creeping up on us. We've got work to do.'

We go back to the middle of the lawn. Gizmo follows us, still seeming a bit peaky after trying that skinny abomination.

'There's one more trick I want to try,' she says.

'Oh yeah, what's that?'

Lib narrows her eyes and smiles. 'Kill.'

I involuntarily gasp.

'Not literally,' she says. 'It just might be a good trick to show how well-trained and protective he is.'

'I don't think he will,' I say. 'I've been trying to get him to do it for years as part of the Intergalactic Power Squad, but he just won't.'

Lib laughs. 'The intergalactic what?'

My face suddenly burns with the heat of a thousand suns and I stare at a patch of dirt on the lawn so it's not too obvious. 'Nothing. I'm just saying, 'I don't think he'll ever do it.'

'We'll see.' Lib picks up Mr Monkey and holds him just off the floor. Gizmo immediately pays attention. Nobody touches Mr Monkey. Mostly because he's so slobbery and disgusting, but also because he's Gizmo's and Gizmo's alone. Lib growls and shakes Mr Monkey backwards and forwards. 'Gizmo, kill!'

Gizmo trots over, pulls Mr Monkey away, and takes him under a table where he kisses him all over.

'There's no way he'll attack Mr Monkey,' I say.

'Do you have anything else?'

I think about it. Oh, actually I do. I run into the house, past Mum and upstairs to my room. I grab a big old teddy bear from my wardrobe and bring it out into the garden.

'Perfect,' says Lib. She whistles Gizmo over and dangles the bear in front of him, growling and lightly batting him in the face.

'Gizmo, kill!'

Gizmo sniffs the bear for a second, then starts kissing it.

'You know what?' says Lib. 'Maybe Gizmo's too nice for the kill command.'

I knew he'd never obey a 'kill' command. Getting

him to dance is one thing, but you can't completely change his personality.

Lib puts the teddy on the table and turns to me. 'Right, I think it's time we started training you up.'

I gulp. This is the bit I was nervous about.

'Remember what I said, George—shoulders back, chin up.'

I do as she says and try to ignore Mum still gawping out of the window, but my commands drift away on the wind like a lonely fart. I try so many times, but I just can't get Gizmo to do anything.

We sit down on Dad's rickety old bench. Gizmo curls up next to us and goes straight to sleep.

'Look George, maybe it's a better idea if I do the show with Gizmo,' she says.

'Oh, would you?' I say, possibly a bit too eagerly.

'It'll probably be for the best,' she says. 'The two of you have had a lifetime of settling into a dynamic where Gizmo's the boss. You can't undo that overnight. He sees me as an authority figure.'

I look up at her. Can't blame him. If you don't know her properly, Lib seems kind of terrifying.

'Don't worry, I don't want the prize money,' she says. 'Cos if it goes well, I can get a promotion at work. And a pay rise.'

'Really?'

'Course,' says Lib. 'A prize-winning dog trainer will be an asset to the Practically Pawfect organization. Even a mad old antique like Sharon will see that.' She ruffles Gizmo's fur and he lets out a long, contented moan. 'Don't worry, Gizmarella, you shall go to the seaside.'

The Rock

I loved the sea so much. I swam in it for ages and never got tired. I felt like I could go for ever. Of course, I had to stop eventually, though. We went back to Mum and Dad and they dried me off with a towel and gave me treats.

Later on, I helped George dig a big pit in the sand which we buried Dad in, leaving just his face sticking out. It was the most I'd ever heard them all laugh.

Before we left to go back to the holiday park, George and I took a walk all the way along the beach, until Mum and Dad looked like two dots on the horizon. At the other end, there was a huge rock. You could have stacked six Georges on top of each other and they still wouldn't reach the top. We stood and watched as a few other kids tried to climb it. They couldn't quite make it though, because parts of it were slippy with seaweed or too steep.

'What do you think of that, Gizmo?' said George. 'Reckon I'd be able to climb it?'

I looked up and let out a little yip. Of course George could climb it. He's Ultra Boy. He can do anything.

George had a go at climbing it, but he couldn't get very far.

'I'm not wearing my Ultra Shoes, Wonder Dog,' he said to me, wriggling his toes in the sand. 'We'll return tomorrow with the correct equipment.'

When we got back to the chalet and I had fought my way through a terrible bath to get all the sand off me, I snuggled with George on his bed while he wrote a brand new short story: 'Ultra Boy Conquers the Space Rock of Zagron'.

When he finished, he read the whole thing to me, only stopping to correct mistakes or change the odd word here and there. He got more and more excited as the story went on. When it was over, and Ultra Boy had claimed the Space Rock in the name of the Intergalactic Power Squad, he lay back on the bed and said, 'I can't wait to do that for real.'

Chapter Twenty-Two

'Duggan!' Mr Brandrick barks from across the car park.

Oh God, what does he want now? If I've learnt anything at this school it's that Brandrick yelling your name is never good news.

'Don't go anywhere, I need a word.' He cocks his head back, signalling for me to go over to him. He's just got out of his car and his arms are full of books, papers, and a takeaway coffee.

I quietly groan and trudge over to him. What's so important that it can't wait until we get into Form? I've started coming into school early so I can avoid crossing paths with Matt and the Morons, but I might have to rethink that strategy if I'm going to get harassed by Brandrick every morning.

When I get over there, he fixes me with his trademark PE teacher glare. The same one he gives you when you score an own goal or nearly impale him with a javelin. 'Everything all right, Duggan?'

'Fine,' I say, as if this is the dinner table and he's my mum.

'I noticed your mate has moved seats in Form.'

Matt relocated to the row at the back the Monday he shoved me. I don't mind. It would have been awkward otherwise. I nod.

'What's happened?'

I shrug. 'We're just not friends any more. No big deal.'

He narrows his eyes at me for a second, then dumps his stuff on the roof of his car, where he has to stop a behaviour report for Ethan from blowing away.

'It happens to some kids,' he says, rummaging through a folder. 'They make the move up to high school and all of a sudden they think they're a big-time Charlie.' He pulls out a sheet of yellow paper, folds it, and passes it to me. 'Don't you go changing though, eh? You'd never hear me admit this in front of the rest of the rabble, but you're all right, Duggan.

Now do me a favour and take that down to Mr Boocock in the PE department. I'd do it but I have a date with this grande cappa-frappa thingy and this month's *Beano*.'

I nod and turn to leave, grumbling under my breath about being nothing but an errand boy, but Brandrick calls me back.

'Remember, Duggan, if there's anything you need to talk about, you know where I am.'

I head down to PE with the note. Man, Brandrick being nice is unsettling. Maybe I could talk to him about stuff? Actually, he'd probably just make me do press-ups until I stop feeling feelings. Forget it. I have a sly read of the paper on my way but it's just a load of teacher mumbo jumbo and nothing juicy.

School has become a bit less stressful now Matt, Tyler, and Ethan have started leaving me alone. It has allowed me to concentrate on the show this weekend. It's only two days away. I'm sure Lib will be brilliant, but I'm still bricking it.

I find Mr Boocock in the office next to the changing rooms. He's moaning and slapping the side of the computer monitor as if that will make it work. When I give him the note he looks at it, shakes his head, and calls Mr Brandrick a 'spanner'.

I leave the office to find a crowd forming outside the girls' changing rooms. They're all laughing and jeering at someone. I'm halfway up the steps when I see their target. Lib. She's holding a bag under her arm and her hair is damp, like she's just got out of the shower.

'About time you had a wash, tramp.'

'What's the matter, don't they have running water on Ampleforth?'

'Don't get too close, she might have fleas.'

She doesn't say or do anything, just tries to push past them. Why is she taking this? Before I can stop myself, I'm running down the stairs.

'Hey, leave her alone!'

They all stare at me, then start laughing.

'You like them young, don't you, tramp?'

'Cradle-snatcher!'

Lib pushes past them and up the stairs. I go after her, but she spins around and yells, 'Leave me alone,' then runs away.

It's like being slapped across the face. Just when I think I understand the world, it knocks me on my back.

Chapter Twenty-Three

'George!' Mum calls up the stairs. 'You have a visitor!'

I groan and drag myself out of bed. If this is Dad, I'm not going to be happy. I start going downstairs but stop halfway when I see who it is.

'All right?' says Lib.

Mum gives me a thin smile and goes into the kitchen. Lib is standing by the front door. She's wearing a black wrestling T-shirt and ripped jeans and she's holding a plastic bag.

'Um, yeah, I think so.'

I don't really know what else to say. She seemed so angry with me yesterday, it kind of shook me up.

'Nice PJs,' she says.

I look down at my superhero pyjamas and blush. I babble something about not expecting visitors on a Saturday morning but Lib's not listening. She reaches into the bag and pulls out a couple of chocolate bars. 'You like Twix?'

I nod and she chucks one to me.

'Thanks.'

'Just wanted to say sorry for yesterday,' she says, kicking the toe of her tatty trainers into the carpet. 'Shouldn't have snapped at you like that.'

'That's OK,' I say. 'You were having a hard time. I know what that's like.'

She nods but doesn't say anything. Should I go down the rest of the stairs? Should I stay where I am? It's weird being above her. I feel like a judge.

'Does that happen a lot?' I ask.

She nods again. 'It's got worse lately cos we're waiting for our shower to be fixed at home so Ms Haroon said I could use the one at school. That makes me a tramp, apparently.' She quickly shakes her head likes she's trying to clear it. 'Anyway, what do we think this is, therapy? Let's do something fun.'

'Like what?'

Lib grins mischievously. 'Like crossing something off Gizmo's list.'

'Sounds good,' I say. 'But shouldn't we rehearse for the show tomorrow?'

'Nah,' says Lib. 'Me and Gizmo have our routine sorted. Any more practising would be overkill at this point. So come on, what's left on the list?'

I think about it. We can't take him to Golden Beach. Not yet. And I'm not sure how we'll go about getting him fifteen minutes of fame. That just leaves the ice cream, the hill, and . . .

'How about we start the calendar?' says Lib. 'We could even get it printed. Get it out there for Christmas, make a bit of money. You've seen them in the shops, right? People will buy any old rubbish.'

I was just planning on keeping it for myself, but that might not be a bad idea. Mum always buys a calendar with all these muscly firemen on it. She says it's because she wants to support the charity. I usually ask why she doesn't support whichever charity makes the nurse calendar but she never answers.

'How are we going to do that?' I ask. 'We don't have a photo studio.'

'Don't we?' says Lib.

We stand outside Practically Pawfect with Gizmo and I feel the early rumblings of a freakout in my belly.

'Are you sure this is a good idea?' I say. 'What if Sharon sees us?'

Lib chuckles and softly punches my arm. 'You worry too much. Besides, she's got wall-to-wall classes today. She wouldn't notice if you strutted through in your superhero pyjamas.'

Using her staff fob to get through the side gate, Lib leads us back to the grooming parlour Gizmo had his pampering session in. The staff in there give us weird looks as we pass through but I try to ignore it. Gizmo growls at a Pomeranian who is having a bath and I drag him out before a riot kicks off. Lib takes a set of keys off her belt and opens a storage cupboard in a staff-only room at the back. Inside are stacks of dog costumes; all sizes, all varieties. You could dress a Great Dane as a Pikachu, no bother.

'We do photo shoots here sometimes,' she says. 'I'll borrow some costumes for ours.'

She goes inside and starts sifting through the boxes. 'We'll need twelve outfits. Ah, perfect.' She holds up a pumpkin jumper. 'How do you like this,

Mr October?' But Gizmo is too busy trying to get back into the parlour so he can start a ruckus with that Pomeranian.

Within a few minutes, Lib has stuffed an armful of dog outfits into a big bag.

'What have you got there?' I jump so high, I nearly stick my head through the ceiling. I turn around and thank every god I can think of that it isn't Sharon. It's a woman wearing the same kind of purple overalls Lib wears when she's working.

'Just doing some washing, Barbara,' says Lib, shaking the bag. 'These costumes are in a horrific state, so I thought I'd take the initiative.'

Barbara scowls at us with a face like a bum sucking a lemon. 'Then why have you got a dog with you? And who's this boy? And how come you're here when you're not due in until next week?'

Lib laughs. 'Someone's feeling question-y, today. This is my little brother, Cuthbert.' She clamps a hand on my shoulder and squeezes it. 'I said I'd show him where his big sis works.' She leans in close to Barbara and whispers, 'He doesn't have many friends.'

I flush bright red and stare at the floor. Lib's told a pack of lies so far, but that last part was a little too close to the truth.

Barbara huffs and shakes her head. 'Whatever. Just hurry up and do what you've got to do.'

Lib watches her stomp away and pulls a face behind her back. When Barbara's finally out of sight, Lib unlocks a door next to the store cupboard and walks through. Gizmo and I follow her. Wow. I wasn't expecting this. There's a wall-length green backdrop, some lights on tall stands, a camera, a laptop, and a big wooden chest. Lib shuts and locks the door behind us.

'Welcome to the photo studio,' she says, firing up the computer. 'Do me a favour and put Gizmo in a costume, will you?'

I rummage through the bag and pull out a bumblebee costume, complete with wobbly antennae. I pull it over Gizmo's head. He grins back at me and gives me a kiss and I can't help but laugh.

'Nice,' chuckles Lib. 'I reckon that'll do nicely for June.' She gets Gizmo to stand in front of the green backdrop, then snaps some photos on the camera.

'OK, get him in the next outfit while I sort these out.' I pull the costume off Gizmo, who is even more excited to see a pair of bunny ears come out.

'These will be great for April,' I say.

'Hey, check this out,' says Lib, pointing at the laptop screen.

I get up to take a look. Ha! She's made it look like bumblebee-Gizmo is sitting in a flower.

'That's brilliant,' I say. 'You're a genius!'

Lib punches my arm. 'Oh, you. It's just a bit of green screen. Easiest thing in the world. Right, get him in position again and I'll see if I can find something Easter-y.

We carry on like this, taking loads more photos. We dress him as a gnome and put him in front of a pond for May. We put him in a cute jumper with flames stitched onto it for November and have him next to a bonfire. We give him a fake rose for February. The big wooden chest is full of props and we find some little fake bushes and clouds. I put some of them on the photos because it's good to have stuff in the foreground. Within a couple of hours, we've done eleven months. We've just got December to do. I'm setting up the fake snow when—

BANG BANG BANG.

I freeze. Even Gizmo, dressed as Santa, looks startled.

'I know you're in there, Lib. Barbara saw you taking costumes.'

Lib puts her finger to her lips. There's no other way out of here besides the way we came in.

'Look, you can either let me in, or I can go back to my office, fetch the key, and come back, but if I have to do that, I will not be happy.'

Even though I can't see her, I can tell Sharon isn't smiling any more. What do we do? Wait a second. I grab Gizmo, tiptoe-run over to the chest, get in, and gently close the lid.

'OK, I'm coming,' says Lib.

I hear the door opening and Sharon walking in. Gizmo's nose is going frantically, trying to locate all the smells. I wish he'd stop.

'Where's the dog? And your brother?'

No, no, no, no.

Lib snorts. 'What dog? What brother?'

'Barbara said she saw you come in here with your brother and a dog.'

I hear footsteps getting closer to the chest.

'All due respect,' says Lib. 'But I think the stress might be getting to Barbara. I mean, I don't even have a brother.'

BOOMPF. Wait, why has it got even darker? Is Lib . . . is Lib sitting on the chest?

'Fine,' says Sharon, more muffled now, 'Even

if there's no brother, that still doesn't explain why you're here, using my equipment, and taking my costumes when you are not due in work today.'

I hold my breath. How would I explain it if I was Lib?

'It's for a school project.'

Sharon sighs. 'You're taking photos of dog costumes for a school project?'

'It's for Art,' says Lib. 'I'm very experimental.'

It goes quiet. Gizmo kisses my chin. Suddenly his tongue seems like the loudest thing since the Big Bang.

'Well that doesn't excuse you using my facilities without permission.'

I hear Lib shuffling slightly. 'Yeah, sorry. I've kind of left it till the last minute and I was going to ask you but I knew you were busy. It won't happen again.'

'It had better not.'

I hear her move towards the door, then stop.

'I stuck my neck out for you, Lib,' says Sharon. 'People said I was mad taking on a girl from Ampleforth, but I told them you were different. Don't make a fool out of me.'

Sharon leaves, slamming the door behind her.

BANG. Something slams on the lid. It might have been Lib's hand. I give it a few seconds before knocking.

'Can we come out?'

Lib gets up and opens the chest. Gizmo jumps out and I follow him, giving him a fuss for being so good at hiding.

Lib clenches her fists and swears, her face red with rage. 'I knew Barbara was a stuck-up old crone but I didn't have her down as a snitch.'

She opens the door a crack. Luckily, the photo studio is close to the gate. She opens it further and looks outside. 'OK, we're clear. Let's go.'

When we finally stop running, I look down at Santa Gizmo, grinning back at me, his beard waving in the breeze. I had no idea this bucket list was going to be so dangerous.

'Should we take this costume back?'

Lib shakes her head. 'I'll return it next week. We still haven't taken the Mr December photo, have we?'

'So where are we going to do that?' I ask Lib.

Lib narrows her eyes and pokes her tongue into the inside of her cheek. 'I think I know the perfect place.'

Chapter Twenty-Four

Tammerstone Snow World squats on the horizon like a sleeping giant. The advert says it's the area's only real-snow ski slope. Despite the fact that I live five minutes down the road, I've only ever been inside once. It was Matt's eighth birthday party and we had a skiing lesson. I kept falling over but the boots were too heavy for me to get back up so I had to wait for the instructor to lift me. It was proper miserable.

Snow World shares a foyer with the swimming pool so there's a heavy chlorine stench hanging over reception, which takes me back to primary school and doing widths of the little pool. We'd sometimes have time to play afterwards, and me and Matt would pretend to be Ultra Boy and AntiMatter Kid on a dangerous mission to the water planet Aquus 5.

'Excuse me?' I turn around and a lady in a Snow World uniform is standing there. 'There's no dogs in here.'

'Yeah there is,' says Lib. 'There's one right here, look. His name's Gizmo.'

The woman clamps her lips together and huffs through her nose. 'I meant there's no dogs allowed.'

Lib sniggers. 'Well then you should have been more specific.' She looks at her badge. 'As it happens, Judy, Gizmo *is* allowed here because he is an assistance dog.'

Judy looks me up and down like I'm the type of thing Gizmo would leave on the pavement. Then her eyes properly focus on Gizmo for the first time and she seems to notice that he's dressed as Santa Claus. In June. 'And what kind of "assistance" does he offer?'

Lib gasps. 'Oh my God, I can't believe you are discriminating against someone with a condition. I am going to write a letter to the Prime Minister.'

Judy tuts and shakes her head. 'Fine,' she grumbles. 'I don't get paid enough for this nonsense.'

I gaze up at Lib in amazement. She can do

anything. And the weird thing is, she doesn't know how close to the truth she is. Gizmo kind of is my assistance dog. Having said all that, I'm still not entirely sure what she has planned and how she's going to do it. We walk across the foyer, past the swimming check-in desk, and down the stairs to the Snow World reception. Lib walks straight past and towards some lockers to the right. I remember this now. You're supposed to get your skiing gear on before heading through the turnstiles onto the slope. We watch as people go through. They all have tickets. It's kind of like what you get at a train station but bigger to accommodate skis.

'So what are we going to do?' I ask her.

Lib taps her chin like she's thinking. 'OK,' she says. 'I've got a plan. Put Gizmo down.'

'What's the plan?' I ask, growing more nervous by the second.

She waves me off. 'If I tell you, you'll overthink it and end up stuffing it up. Just follow my lead, all right?'

She's got a point, I suppose. I put Gizmo down and scratch the back of his ear. His nose is twitching like mad at all the new smells—the chlorine drifting down from the pool, people's clothes all wet from the snow, the hot drinks and pastries on sale at the snack bar. Lib watches the turnstiles as if she's picking her moment. When the queue dies down, she whistles. Gizmo's attention snaps straight to her. She grabs a treat out of her pocket and holds it up. Gizmo's eyes lock onto it like it's the One Ring and he's Gollum. Before he can make a grab for it, Lib launches it over the turnstiles and onto the slope. Without a second's hesitation, Gizmo takes off across the reception area and skids under the barrier and out onto the snow. We run after him until we get to the barrier.

'Gizmo, stop!' Lib shouts. Gizmo hits the brakes and spins around. If he goes much further, he'll be in the path of skiers. Lib nudges me in the ribs. 'Quick, take some photos on your phone.'

My hands are shaking, so it's hard to zoom in, but I manage it eventually. A small crowd has started to gather.

'Isn't he the most adorable thing you've ever seen?'

'Aww, look at the little cutie pie, he thinks it's Christmas!'

'Hey!' a big, hairy security guard with a huge beard yells. 'Whose dog is this?'

'Keep snapping,' Lib mumbles to me, before

turning her attention to the man. 'I'm so sorry. He's our assistance dog. Not assisting us very well at the moment, is he? OK, come on then, boy!'

I get one more photo of him, his Santa hat standing on end and his face bright and cheerful. He looks like he's having the time of his life. And if that's not the whole point of the list then what is?

Gizmo bounds through the snow, back through the turnstiles, and shakes himself, sending powdery flakes flying everywhere.

'Don't let it happen again, or I'll have you thrown out,' says the man.

I pick up Gizmo and rub his legs to warm him up. He kisses me all over my face. Lib salutes. 'Terribly sorry, my yeti friend.'

The bloke shouts, 'You what?' But Lib is leading us away, laughing her head off. 'This is the best day ever,' she says.

I think she might be right.

'That didn't take as long as I thought it would,' says Lib as we head back into the foyer. 'What's say we tick another item off the list?' She nods at something in the distance through the window.

'Um...'

MAKE A CALENDAR ✓

The Hill

The hill always loomed over us. Literally. You can see it from miles away. It was always one of those places George said he'd take me, but we never got around to it. Until one day.

George was eleven and I was twelve. That's roughly sixty-nine in dog years. Mum and Dad were arguing again. This was a regular occurrence since the incident. This argument was a little different, though. Dad had been gone for about a week. He'd come back to pick up some things, but of course it turned into a fight.

We sat under the covers on George's bed and waited for it to stop, just like we always did. George scratched behind my ear and sighed. 'They're arguing over who gets the bedroom TV. Should I be offended that they haven't argued over who gets me yet?'

We waited some more but they didn't stop. They just got louder and angrier. The topic then turned to the incident, as it always did. Attacking each other about it. Blaming each other.

Then Dad said something new. Something which made George gasp.

'It's been nearly two years. Shouldn't he have got over it by now?'

George picked me up and took me downstairs. I thought he was going to go into the living room and join in the shouting, but instead we went straight into the kitchen and outside, only stopping to pick up my lead.

We didn't walk the usual way. I didn't even get to go past Reginald's house and tell him what I thought of him. We headed straight for the big hill. George didn't speak much, he just wiped his eyes with his sleeve and put his hood up.

It took us a long time to get up there and when we finally did, I was pretty tired. I lay down in the grass so I could get my breath back. George sat next to me.

I'd never been so high before. You could see for miles. The lamp post at the end of our road—the place where I do basically all my wees—looked tiny.

We had been sitting there for a long time when Mum appeared over the brow of the hill. George asked how she knew where to find him and she said, 'Why did you think I let you have that iPhone? Location services, mate.'

She sat down next to me and put her arm around George. His breathing went all jerky and his face started leaking. He said, 'I'm trying to stop it, Mum. I really am. I'm sorry. All this is because of me.'

Mum made 'shhhh' noises and told him he had nothing to be sorry for. And I'm not a human and I don't understand these things, but I've got a feeling George didn't really believe her.

Chapter Twenty-Five

'So,' says Lib, as we wind our way up the path. 'What's so special about this hill?'

Gizmo stops to sniff a lamp post. 'I just like it,' I say.

'Yeah, but why's it on the list?'

I cough even though I don't need to. 'Did you know this is actually a man-made hill?' I say. 'It's what's technically known as a slag heap.'

Lib laughs. 'Well, that's taken some of the magic out of it.'

The sun is peeking out from behind the clouds and I'm starting to sweat. The walk is taking longer than I thought because Gizmo insists on stopping for a wee at every opportunity, like he's trying to claim the hill in his name. I guess that's the big difference between humans and dogs. When humans want to take territories they fight and die and the winner sticks a flag in it. Dogs just do a wee.

We're about three quarters of the way up when Gizmo stops for good. He's put the brakes on, thrown out the anchor. He's not walking any further. It's been a tiring day. He's been walking, posed for a photo shoot, frolicked in the snow. It's like a whole year of stuff condensed into a few hours. I pick him up and carry on. Not much further now, and we'll get there quicker without all the pee breaks.

When we reach the top, I put Gizmo down, take a bottle of water out of my bag, and tip it out so he can have a drink. He laps it straight out of the bottle like it's a hosepipe. We sit down on the grass and look out at the town below. I can appreciate it more this time because my eyes aren't all streamy. It's like a model village; the tiny shops, cars, and buses, the ant-like people going about their business. From up here it's easy to forget that that's where life happens. Where everything seems so important and up-close. If I could see this view when Matt, Ethan, and Tyler are bothering me, or when Dad is trying to install Rosa as some sort of second Mum, I'd realize it's not that big a deal. We're all just small parts of a big machine.

Gizmo lies down next to me and I ruffle his fur. It has more grey flecks in it than last time we were up here. Lib sits the other side. 'I can see why you wanted to come up here. Pretty, isn't it? I mean, not the town itself. The town is basically the devil's bum, but when you zoom out like this, it's all right.'

The sun is low and orange, sending beautiful beams of light over the church and the castle and, you know, Snow World. I can see my house at the end of the cul-de-sac. I can see Dad's flat at the other end of town. From up here, the distance is only the length of my arm. Gizmo sighs heavily. That's always a sign he's properly falling asleep. Soon, his legs will start kicking and he might even bark a little.

Lib leans back on her arms and basks in the sunlight. 'It's like escape,' she says, and I know exactly what she means.

We don't say anything for a while. Gizmo nudges my leg with his paws and his tail beats the floor a couple of times. I'm glad I put this on the list. I feel like I can come back here now.

'I was reading a book the other day,' says Lib,

breaking the silence.

'Oh yeah? What was it about?'

'Fossils and stuff,' she says. 'I'm well into things like that. Science. Why things are the way they are. Anyway, I was reading about how scientists found these mosquitoes from millions of years ago preserved in amber.'

'I thought that was just a thing from *Jurassic Park*.'

'It is,' says Lib. 'But it's real, too. I just thought it was mad that you can preserve something so fragile for so long. I've not been able to get it out of my head.'

I scratch behind Gizmo's ear and watch his eyelids flutter as he sleeps.

'It's a shame we can't do that for real—with memories, I mean,' I say, my mind flicking back to the moment I'd preserve in amber. On Golden Beach. Before the incident. Before Dad left. Before Matt changed. Before Gizmo got old.

'Kind of,' says Lib. 'But being trapped in amber for ten million years doesn't sound so great either. We're supposed to change, George. Even if it's painful.'

We sit quietly again and look out at a field on

the horizon where they're building a big estate of new posh houses. In quiet moments you can hear the rumble of the dumpers and the beeps of the reversing trucks.

I don't know how long we've been sitting there when Lib stands up and stretches. 'I've really got to go now. This has been fun, though. I'll see you tomorrow for the show, yeah?' She reaches down and fusses Gizmo, who wakes up for a second, wags his tail, then immediately goes back to sleep.

'Bye, Lib,' I say, waving her off.

According to films and stuff like that, you're supposed to offer to walk girls home, but even asking that would be ridiculous. Me walking Lib home would be like a chihuahua being a bodyguard for a Rottweiler.

I scan the horizon until I see Ampleforth Drive, where Lib is heading. I remember when I used to think everyone that lived there was dangerous and to be avoided, but now I see that's a load of rubbish.

I'll stay here a little while longer before I head home. The air is cleaner up here—no car fumes or smog from the industrial estate. I take a big gulp of it and scratch behind Gizmo's ear. He murmurs contentedly and his eyelids flutter. He needs plenty of sleep so he's rested for his big day tomorrow. I gaze into the horizon, right where the land meets the sky. I'm glad we came up here again.

CLIMB THE BIG HILL ✓

Chapter Twenty-Six

Is it normal to be this nervous at a dog show? I look around and everyone seems really chilled, but I feel like I'm about to leap out of a plane.

There's a big canvas sign stretched between two poles near the farm entrance that says 'Tammerstone Cross-Breed Dog Show'. I've already signed up and have the itinerary in my hands. Gizmo will be in the medium dogs' heat, then if he gets through that, the semi-final, and after that, the final. My heat starts at ten-thirty, which is . . . I check my watch . . . only twenty minutes away. Huh. Lib should be here by now. We agreed to meet at the signing-in desk at ten. She must be running late.

Gizmo is loving it here. He seems to like the

look of this huge black dog, probably a Great Dane cross, and keeps wanting to go over and play. The big dog (named Norma) wasn't really into Gizmo as much and shook him off like an over-enthusiastic flea. The owner is a nice old bloke who was impressed I'm into dog shows at such a young age. I didn't have the heart to tell him I'm only here because I want to win the money so I can take Gizmo on holiday.

Where is Lib, though? I keep watching the dirt track that leads to the farm but there's no sign of her. I try calling her but it clicks straight through to voicemail. Weird.

I decide to take my mind off things and watch the small dogs' heat. If Gizmo gets through, he'll probably be facing the winners of this so I should be keeping an eye on the competition, anyway. There are all kinds of different dogs and the best thing about it being crosses only is that they all have their own characters. There's one dog with different-coloured eyes, there's another one with really strange markings on its fur. I sneak a Jammie Dodger out of my bag and give half to Gizmo. I bought a pack on the way here. Gizmo demolishes the half in about two seconds, then looks at me for more.

'Later,' I say.

Gizmo huffs before flinging himself to the ground and rolling in the dirt.

I watch how the heat is going. The judge goes around the dogs one by one and checks them over, then gets them to walk in a circle. I can manage that if Lib is running late. How hard can it be?

No, she's going to be here. There's no way she'll bail on me. We've been through too much.

But I don't know her. Not really. All she's told me about herself is that she lives in Ampleforth Drive with her mum and she doesn't have a dog. That's it. She could have just been winding me up the whole time. Stringing along the stupid Year Eight kid. It could be like Casey's party all over again.

I shake my head quick and take a few deep breaths. That won't happen. Stop thinking the sky's falling in, George. Get a grip.

When I come to my senses, the judge has awarded first, second, and third prizes. They'll all go through to the semi. I think the winner was a little Jackadoodle. The loudspeaker crackles into life.

'Congratulations Poppy, Luther, and Muffin. Now can the medium category competitors please make their way to the arena?'

Brick in my throat. And possibly my pants. Where. Is. Lib? I try to call her again, but it's as if her phone is switched off. We slowly make our way over. I keep looking around for her, but she's nowhere. And she definitely wouldn't blend in with this crowd.

The judge takes my competitor number and asks me to join the line-up. I'm standing next to what looks like a Cockapoo. Its owner, a lady in a hairy pink jumper, keeps sniffing and it's really getting on my nerves.

Calm down, George. Calm down. You'll probably never see any of these people again, so even if you do fall flat on your face with your trousers around your ankles, it won't matter.

Why won't my stupid brain ever SHUT UP? Look, you'll be fine. You saw the first heat. All you have to do is keep Gizmo standing up nice and straight and walk with him in a circle. A sleepy chimp could do it.

I look along the line. There are some really smart dogs here. The kind of dogs that look like they've actually been groomed. I reach down and pick a leaf out of Gizmo's fur.

'Are you going to be a good boy?' I ask him. He looks back at me as if to say, 'Of course I am, you numpty.' Then he lies on the floor and starts eating the grass.

'The judge is about to begin her deliberation,' goes the loudspeaker. I gently encourage Gizmo to stand up straight and I remove the last few stray bits of grass from his mouth.

As the judge gets closer, my heart rate rises. With my spare hand, I do my finger exercises. I notice someone taking photos of the line-up but I don't acknowledge it. I just stare straight ahead. How could Lib do this to me?

Before I know it, the judge is in front of me. The normal, logical part of my brain knows she's just a kind old lady who looks a bit like my great-aunt Sheila, but the mad fireworks part of my brain sees a three-headed monster that shoots lava out of its face. I blink hard and take a breath as the monster adjusts its bifocals.

'Gizmo,' it says. 'What a charming name.'

Wow, she even sounds like my great-aunt Sheila. This calms me down a bit and slowly I drift back down to reality like a feather.

'Thank you,' I say.

The judge runs her hand the length of Gizmo's spine. Then she lifts up his tail and nods. I'm not sure what she's nodding at but I'm too scared to ask. Then she pulls back his lips and looks at his teeth. I hope she likes them. I spent twenty minutes this morning trying to clean them. She nods again and moves onto the next dog. That wasn't so bad. I give Gizmo the other half of his Jammie Dodger as a treat for being so well behaved.

After she's inspected the whole line, the judge stands at the front and says, 'OK, parade around the arena, please.' 'Arena' makes it sound grander than it really is. It's just a circle in a field. But hearing the word makes me imagine I'm standing in front of eighty thousand screaming fans at Wembley. She points at the first dog and they lead the way. I watch the two in front of me and see how they're doing it. If I'd known I was going to be doing it myself, I might have prepared in advance.

I bunch the lead up tight in my hand so Gizmo is close, and copying the two women in front, do this weird half-walk half-jog. Gizmo breaks into a trot and wags his tail. After we've been round twice, the judge stops us. She points at the dog next to me:

'First.' She points at a dog at the other end of the row: 'Second.' Wait, is this it? Are we out already? 'Third!' I look up from Gizmo and see she's pointing right at us. We're through! I give Gizmo a big hug and he kisses me like he knows what's happening. We're one step closer to the money!

While they prepare the arena for the next heat, I make my way back to the entrance to see if Lib has arrived. I imagine she'll probably be really embarrassed because she slept in or something like that. No. Still not here. A mixture of anger and worry swirls in my gut. What if she's in some kind of trouble? Anything can happen down Ampleforth Drive.

I go out onto the main road to see if I can see Lib coming. There's nothing but the occasional car rolling past. I send her a text asking if she's on the way. Then I call again. Still goes straight to voicemail. I stand there waiting for about half an hour but there's no sign of her. She's not coming, is she?

Chapter Twenty-Seven

It's the semi-final. The judge, a different one this time, has inspected Gizmo and we've done the walk around. But now there's something extra. The obstacle course. I thought the idea was whichever dog went through it the quickest is the winner, but it's more about how well they do it. Still, Gizmo loves obstacle courses. He'll be fine. I hope.

There are four dogs in our semi—a small, two mediums, and a large. There are two different obstacle courses, with the large dogs having their own. Makes sense, really. There's no way Gizmo's mate Norma is going to fit on this see-saw.

It looks like Gizmo is going to be last up. So far, the others have done pretty well. A Yorkie cross knocked a couple of cones over but other than that, not bad.

'OK,' says the judge, squinting at his clipboard. 'Next up, Gizmo.'

I unclip Gizmo's lead and ruffle his fur. 'Go and get 'em,' I whisper. He doesn't need any encouragement from me though, and he tears into the obstacle course like he's trying to qualify for the Dog Olympics. As we reach the end, I get half a Jammie Dodger out ready, but Gizmo tears past me and goes through the large dogs' obstacle course as well. Everyone laughs, even the judge. When I finally get Gizmo back, he's panting like mad and has to have a drink out of the communal arena tub.

The judge stands in front of us, rubbing his beardy chin. I hope Gizmo's extra run-around hasn't disqualified him. The judge extends his finger and my stomach wrings itself out like an old tea towel. 'First!' He points at Norma. 'Second!' He points at Gizmo.

What?! We're through to the final! Gizmo jumps up my legs and I give him another Jammie Dodger half. This is amazing! I can't believe Gizmo is through to the final of a dog show. The world has gone insane.

It's going to be tough, though. And I don't know if I can do it without Lib. In all my attempts to get Gizmo to do tricks, Gizmo has never done a thing. Lib's right—I don't have enough confidence.

I scrape together enough money from the change in my pocket to buy a hot dog from the van, which I split with Gizmo. I put my arm around him as he eats. 'At least you'll always be my friend, Gizmo,' I say. There's no way he'd get too cool for me, or stand me up. I swallow the bowling ball lump in my throat. It was nice having a human friend for a while, though.

A collie cross comes bounding over to Gizmo. I

can't see her owner nearby. She sniffs at him and he tenses up. He must not like her as much as Norma. His tail is standing on end with the tip curled over like a question mark. A low growl builds up in his throat.

'Gizmo, no,' I say, but he ignores me. That's not good. He's supposed to be obeying my every command. The growl gets louder and the other dog bares its teeth. I stand up and try to lead Gizmo away but the dog snaps at him and Gizmo snaps back. 'No!' I say, but it doesn't work. Luckily, the noise attracts the attention of the dog's owner, who apologetically collects her. Gizmo is shaken, I can tell. I crouch down and fuss him, tell him it'll be all done soon. He peppers my face with hot-dog flavoured kisses.

What was that? Something just bounced off the back of my head. Is it that dog back for round two? I get up and turn around.

'Hello, freakshow.'

Chapter Twenty-Eight

'We were just in the woods,' says Matt. 'And Ethan
said he thought he saw you at the dog show. I said,
"No way. George is a saddo but he's not that sad."
But it looks like I'm wrong. If you'd told us, we'd
have been here from the start, wouldn't we, lads?'

I say nothing. I can't. My throat is too choked. I
just walk away. What were they doing in the woods?
Harassing squirrels? This is just my luck. The
loudspeaker crackles into life.

'The final of the Tammerstone Cross-Breed Dog
Show will begin in five minutes. Can all competitors
please make their way to the arena?'

I head straight down there, the sarcastic whoops
and cheers of the stupid ManDem ringing in my

ears. I am placed at the end. The crowd gathers around the edge. Everyone is here for the final. I just wish *they* weren't. They're standing off to the side, pulling faces at me. I turn away and check on Gizmo. He still seems a little freaked out from his encounter with the collie cross.

'Congratulations on reaching the final,' says the judge. 'We have already seen the dogs' conditioning, their walking, and their obstacle course ability, so there is only one thing left to judge—their obedience.'

Oh no. My head pounds. Beads of sweat begin to form on my forehead like condensation on a car window. I've never been able to do any of this. The obedience stuff is the entire reason Lib was supposed to be on board. I can't do it!

First dog is up. It's a labradoodle called Murphy. He sits, begs, and rolls over perfectly. Big round of applause.

The second dog is what looks to me like a cross between a Shar Pei and a cocker spaniel—all soft fur and baggy skin. It does an even neater job than the first one and even throws in a little spin.

The third dog is Norma. Gizmo's ears prick up when he sees her. She's ridiculously well-coordinated for such a gangly dog.

With every passing second, I grow more nervous. I try and centre myself, as Dr Kaur used to say, but it doesn't help. I couldn't be less centred if all my body parts were spread across the Andromeda Galaxy.

OK, we're up. Matt, Tyler, and Ethan start a sarcastic 'George' chant. I try to ignore them but it's too loud. Eventually, the judge has to get on the loudspeaker and ask them to be quiet.

I step to the front and face Gizmo. I try to speak but my voice doesn't work. I clear my throat and try again.

'Gizmo, sit.' It comes out in a rasp and even with his sensitive dog hearing, there's no way Gizmo will have heard it.

'Are you OK?' the judge asks.

Oh my God, this is going horribly. Gizmo looks up at me, his tongue hanging out the side of his mouth. 'Gizmo,' I manage to croak out louder. 'Sit.'

Gizmo sniffs the ground, then starts trying to chew his own leg.

'He's bottled it!' Tyler yells. Matt and Ethan laugh and clap.

I really don't have the confidence for this. I'm useless. A loser. I eye up the exit. If I pick up Gizmo and run, I could be out of here in less than a minute.

But what about Golden Beach? Don't I want Gizmo to at least have a fair shot of getting there? Don't I want him to swim in the sea, play on the sand, and have a delicious ice cream from the van? Don't I want to look all my problems straight in the eye once and for all? Why should my stupid brain stop that from happening? When it tells me I'm not good enough, I need to shut it up and say, 'Yes I am!' I might not be cool or interesting enough for Matt, but I'm good enough to exist.

I picture the view from the top of the hill. I see the farm from above—how small we must all look from there. I'm not scared any more.

'Gizmo,' I say. 'Sit!'

Gizmo sits down. Everyone apart from the ManDem bursts into a massive round of applause, probably because they're so relieved.

'Gizmo, lie down.'

Gizmo lies down.

'Gizmo, roll over.'

Gizmo rolls over and jumps back to his feet.

'Gizmo, spin.'

Gizmo spins twice.

'Gizmo, beg.'

Gizmo sits up on his hind legs and begs with both paws. I throw him a quarter of a Jammie Dodger. We're on a roll. We're doing it. I glance over at Matt through the cheering and clapping crowd and he's watching stone-faced with his arms folded.

'Gizmo, follow me.'

I turn around and Gizmo jumps up and follows me as I walk, both of us on two legs. The cheering gets louder.

'Gizmo, dance!'

Gizmo, still on his hind legs, moves backwards and forwards and spins around. I touch the tip of his paw so it looks like I'm twirling him. The crowd go wild. We've done it! No matter what happens, we've proved that we can do whatever we want, just the two of us. Confidence? Schmonfidence! I've got it in spades, mate. I flash Matt my best grin and blast him with a double thumbs up. I'm enjoying it so much I don't immediately notice the ribbon pinned to my shirt. #1.

'WHAT?!'

'You've won!' the judge says with a grin. 'Congratulations!'

I . . . I can't believe it! I give Gizmo a big kiss and lift him high. Everyone claps and loads of people rush over to congratulate us. Even Norma comes over and nuzzles Gizmo a bit. He does that magical Gizmo smile as the ManDem stomp towards the exit.

'You should be very proud,' the judge says to me.

And I am. I really am.

Chapter Twenty-Nine

I had to get Mum to come down to claim my
winnings for me. Apparently, they can't just hand
envelopes of cash over to thirteen-year-olds or
something, I don't know. I chose Mum over Dad
because I knew she'd be cooler with it. Dad might
have lectured me about putting it in a savings
account or something boring like that, but Mum was
just thrilled. Well, she practically had to be picked
up off the floor when she found out Gizmo was the
most obedient dog in the show.

I asked if I could use the money
to book us a trip to Golden Beach
and she was all like, 'It's your money,
we'll spend it however you like. As long as

you're sure it's a good idea.'

When we get home and Gizmo has a triumphant reunion with Mr Monkey, I go up to my room. Whenever I'm somewhere with lots of people, I need time to myself afterwards to calm down and sort my head out. And when it's something as stressful as the dog show was, I need even more time.

I sit on my bed and close my eyes, doing a breathing exercise Dr Kaur showed me. When I come out of it, I find my brain has drifted from the victory of the dog show to something else—Lib. Why didn't she turn up? She was so excited about the show. She wanted to use it as a way of getting a promotion at work. I'm not as angry now; more worried. The problem is, I don't know where she lives and she's still not answering her phone or replying to texts. There's only one person I can think of that might know how to get hold of her.

I get out my phone and take a long, deep breath. Here we go.

'Practically Pawfect, Sharon speaking. How may I help you?'

I clear my throat and try to do an old man voice. 'Um, hello. I was wondering if Lib was at work presently.'

The line goes quiet. In the background, I hear a dog barking.

'You're that boy, aren't you?' Sharon says, her voice low and flat.

How did she know?!

'No, this is—'

'Don't insult my intelligence, you little twerp,' she snaps. 'I know exactly who you are and what you've been up to.'

'W—what do you mean?'

'You know exactly what I mean—sneaking onto my property and using my facilities for free, when I *told* you to stay away.'

'Buh—buh—buh.'

'Don't even think about lying to me. When I caught that girl in the photo studio yesterday, I knew something was off, so I decided to check all my CCTV footage. Well don't I feel like a fool? Despite my better judgement, I trusted her and she's goes and humiliates me. Never again.'

My skin goes cold and prickly. My mouth flaps open and shut like a broken gate in a hurricane. I can't speak.

'To answer your original question, that girl is not

here because I dismissed her this morning.'

Oh no. Even though she complained about Sharon, Lib loved that job. And she said she needed the money, too.

'I—I'm sorry,' I stammer, but she cuts me off.

'I don't want to hear from any more ungrateful children,' she booms. 'I should have known better than employing scumbags from Ampleforth. Goodbye!' And with that she hangs up.

This can't be happening. Lib has lost her job and it's all because of me.

Chapter Thirty

Lib didn't show up to school today. Now I'm worried about her. Really worried. What if her mum found out she'd been sacked and did something horrible to her? Or what if she ran away? I need to find her and make sure she's OK.

The problem is, I don't know where she lives. I just know it's somewhere on Ampleforth Drive. But there must be about three hundred addresses down there. I never saw her with any other friends so there's not even anyone I can ask.

After school, I pick up Gizmo and head straight over there. I'll find her somehow. I have to. It's colder today, but I don't mind because it will help keep me awake. I probably slept for about an hour last night.

I couldn't stop thinking about Lib.

We filter through the crowds like fish squeezing through a gap in a net and make our way to Ampleforth. To me, it doesn't look that bad. Sure, a couple of the houses are boarded up, but so what? It's just ordinary people living their lives. I bet the people that complain about this place never actually come down here.

Gizmo tugs at the lead and huffs out through his nose. I know what that is—that's the international Gizmo sign for 'cat'. I see it ahead of us, peeking around the side of a wheelie bin. I'd normally change course but Gizmo is too close and is dragging me over to start a ruckus. The cat creeps out, its back arched and its black fur standing up like it's been electrocuted. They usually run away, but this one is going nowhere. Gizmo looks up at me like, 'What is this guy's problem?' I don't think he knows what to do now he's face-to-face with the toughest cat in town.

'Damian!' A yell comes from the house at the end of the path. 'Get in here, you menace!'

A woman with green hair is leaning around her front door. The cat gives Gizmo one last threatening look before slinking back towards the house.

'Sorry about that, my love. He's a tough cookie.'

'That's OK,' I say. 'Actually, can you help me?'

Damian jumps onto the top of an electric meter box so the lady can fuss him.

'What's the matter?' she says. 'Not come to convert me, have you?'

I laugh nervously. 'No, I'm looking for someone. Her name's Lib.'

The lady frowns. 'Don't know anyone by that name. What does she look like?'

'She's tall, half of her head is shaved. About fifteen.'

The lady's eyes dart from side to side like she's watching a tennis match. 'Ah! Now you mention it, that does ring a bell. I reckon she lives in one of the blocks opposite here. Don't know which one, though.'

I say thanks to the lady and drag Gizmo away from Damian the danger cat. Over the road there are three blocks of flats built around a courtyard with a ramshackle kids' play area in it. Each block is three storeys high with open landings. I scan them for clues but there's nothing. What was I expecting? A personalized 'Lib' beach towel hanging over a railing? I'm going to have to take a closer look.

The first block is called Townsend House. There are buzzers which you're supposed to press to get someone to let you in, but someone has propped the door open with a brick.

I go inside. The foyer smells like bleach and cigarette smoke, and there's a wet-floor sign propped up against the wall. I climb the stairs to the top and scout the landings on each floor. Gizmo has to stop for a breather for a few minutes so I leave him by some railings and have another look, just in case I've missed something. Oh, it's useless. I don't even know what I'm looking for. I need to ask someone if they know her. We go back down the stairs and approach the next block, Peel House. There's a man just ahead. He scans a panel on the wall with his key ring and walks in. I jog to catch up with him and grab the open door. He turns and looks at me. He looks kind of like my great-uncle Bernard, with a furry white moustache.

'You here to see someone?' he asks in what I reckon is a Polish accent.

'I think so,' I say. 'I'm looking for a girl called Lib—tall, shaved head.'

The old man frowns and scratches his head under his hat. 'I think I've seen her in the next block—

Hamilton House.'

I thank him and get on my way but the Hamilton House main door is locked. Just my luck. The panel on the wall has about fifteen buttons, each with its own number. It runs from 280 to 294. She could be any of them. I've got a one-in-fifteen chance, I suppose. I take a deep breath. Eeny, meeny, miny, moe. I press 289.

'Hello?' A gruff voice fizzes out of the speaker.

I clear my throat. 'Um, hi. I'm looking for Lib.'

'Yeah and I'm looking for a winning lottery ticket. Sod off.' The line goes dead. Charming.

I try 280. No answer. None at 281 either. 282 is somehow even ruder than 289. I hear plastic bags rustling behind me. Ah good. I might be able to sneak in with whoever this is. Gizmo spins around and barks happily, tugging on the lead like mad. I turn around.

'What are you doing here, George?'

It's Lib, but she looks different. Her eyes are red and puffy and her skin is almost grey.

'Just wanted to check if you're OK,' I say.

Lib lets out a hollow laugh. 'Not really. Hang about down here for a sec, will you? I need to take this shopping up.'

She opens the door and stomps up the stairs, dragging three stuffed shopping bags. I hope she's not dodging me again. I can imagine her going up and not coming back down. I prop myself up on a handrail and wait. Thankfully, she comes back. Without a word, she walks past us and into the play area. Someone has scrawled 'ManDem 4 Life' across the slide in marker pen. Lib sits on a metal bench and folds her arms. I sit next to her despite the fact that it's the most uncomfortable thing in the world. Why do they make benches like this? It's like sitting on a colander. Gizmo takes advantage of my loosened grip and trots over to the roundabout, gently spinning in the wind. He loves those things, even though they make him sick.

Lib stares into the distance. Eventually, she speaks.

'Sorry I didn't make the show. I saw Gizmo won.'

'That's OK,' I say. 'Sorry you lost your job.'

Lib blinks slowly and her chin trembles. 'I'm in trouble, George.'

'Why?'

Lib sighs and looks at me with wet eyes. 'I'm the only one earning money in my house. My mum's poorly.'

Oh. So much stuff makes sense now. Working all those shifts, having to get home, the way she'd always change the subject when any personal stuff came up.

'I have to cook and clean, I have to do the shopping, and I have to work,' she says. 'And I'm supposed to fit school in there somehow, as well.' A tear rolls down her cheek.

'I'm sorry,' I say. 'Why didn't you tell me earlier?'

Lib sniffs. 'I don't know. Ashamed, I guess. I didn't want you to think I'm some kind of tramp like everyone else does.'

I pluck up the courage to touch her shoulder. 'I'd never think that.'

Lib smiles bitterly. 'I wish more people were like you. I have no friends my own age. I could never go to after-school stuff or parties when people asked. In the end, I stopped getting invited and everyone thought I was a loner. Then when they found out I had to shower at school because ours doesn't work, that was it. Game over. With you and Gizmo, at least I could pretend to be normal for a bit. Gizmo's list gave me something fun to focus on.' She stops and runs her hand down her face. 'I don't know what I'm supposed to do, now. Nowhere else is going to give a job to a fifteen-year-old. Sharon was the only game in town.'

'We'll think of something,' I say. 'I promise.'

At which point, Gizmo comes staggering over, and walks straight into the side of an overflowing bin. Looks like even seventy-eight-year-olds still get sick from roundabouts. It also looks like I'm carrying him all the way home.

Chapter Thirty-One

My head's been spinning like a UFO for days. I can't concentrate at school. I can't get excited about Gizmo's list. Mum asked if I wanted her to book our little holiday to Golden Beach but I said no. Not yet. How could I really go there knowing that Lib and her mum are struggling? I've made up my mind.

I grab Gizmo's lead off his hook and while I'm there, I take the envelope with the dog show winnings out of the cupboard.

'I'm sorry, boy,' I say to Gizmo as we walk up our street. 'But they need it more than us. We'll get there some other way.'

Gizmo doesn't seem too bothered. He's more interested in continuing his blood feud with

Reginald, who's going insane on his windowsill.

I try not to think about what I'm giving away. It's only money. Just paper, if you think about it. Besides, do I really want to tick so many things off Gizmo's list? What happens when we've done everything? Gizmo still has plenty of time. I should slow down.

Speaking of which, Gizmo has dropped his pace a bit. To begin with, I thought it was because he was taking in all the new smells on this new route, but now I can see he's plodding a little. Makes sense. Mum has slightly relaxed the diet as a reward for winning the dog show and he's been allowed some proper food. He's probably not used to it. I slow down too but I'm anxious to deliver the envelope as quickly as possible. I don't really want to be carrying four hundred quid down Ampleforth Drive after dark.

We finally arrive at Hamilton House and thankfully, the main door is unlocked. We get to the stairs and Gizmo puts the brakes on. He looks up at them like they're Mount Everest. I'll have to pick him up.

I remember seeing Lib's flat number on her

keys—285, second floor. I walk along the landing and hear sounds drifting out of the flats—music, TV, frying pans sizzling. Gizmo's nose twitches. I bet when you have a really good sense of smell, new places can be overwhelming.

I'm not going to knock. She might talk me out of it. I take the envelope out of my pocket, and before I can question whether it's a good idea or not, stuff it through the letter box and walk away as fast as I can.

I stroke Gizmo on my way down the stairs. 'We've done the right thing, haven't we, boy?'

He stares at me with sad eyes. Great, now I feel terrible.

Look, as I was saying, we'll still get to Golden Beach and we will be helping Lib and her mum out. This was definitely the right thing to do.

A Marine-Based Adventure

When Mum and Dad asked George what he wanted to do on the second day of our holiday, he wasted no time in telling them: he wanted to go back to the beach. He had the whole day planned out.

We got our usual spot on the beach and put our towels down. Dad was in a good mood so he paid to hire a couple of deckchairs for them to sit on.

Meanwhile, George and I started working on the Intergalactic Power Squad's sand base. I dug a massive hole and George used the sand to start constructing a mound. He said he had to use the sand I dug up because it was damp and would stick together just right. I was a good boy that day. Then, he used a bucket to make buildings to go on top. He found some sticks and seaweed and used them to spell out IPS next to it.

'OK, Wonder Dog,' he said to me. 'Now our sand base is complete, we can commence operations. But before we conquer the Space Rock of Zagron we have some important marine-based work to do.' And with that, he picked up a stick and ran down to the sea with me trailing behind him.

Even though I love George, he is still a human and so is as deceptive as the rest of them. That's what I thought when he pretended to throw the stick into the sea and I went barrelling in there after it. When I realized what had happened, I turned back and shook myself all over him. That showed him.

'OK, Wonder Dog,' he said to me. 'Race you.' And he launched the stick into the sea, then sprinted in, sending water splashing up behind him. Of course, dogs have four legs rather than humans' puny two, so I easily beat him and plunged into the deeper water, the stick clamped between my teeth.

George laughed and ducked under the waves. For a second, I was scared because I didn't know where he'd gone, but then he jumped up behind me with a roar!

'I am the Aqua Beast of Rangifango and I'm coming to get you, Wonder Dog!'

I swam back to shore and waited for George to follow me. He eventually lunged out of the water and collapsed in the sand, laughing.

'You're too quick for me, boy,' he said.

Chapter Thirty-Two

Don't rise to it, George. Just eat this horrible chicken and mushroom pie and let them carry on. They're just annoyed because they turned up to laugh at you at the dog show and you won and rubbed it right in their stupid ManDem mushes. Ignore the chips landing on your head. If they want to waste precious food, that's on them.

I calmly put my knife and fork down, carry my tray over to the hatch, and leave the hall. They might be following me and calling me 'Pedigree Chump' and names of that nature, but I'm not bothered. I'm especially no longer bothered that my former best friend I did everything with is calling me a loser. Not at all. We turn the corner at the end of the corridor and run straight into Lib. Oh thank God, she's going to save me. It's going to be like the library all over again. She's going to grab Matt and—WAIT, WHY IS SHE GRABBING ME?

Before I know what to do, she's holding me against the wall with her forearm, digging her elbow into my shoulder.

'Listen, mate,' she breathes. 'I am not a charity case, do you understand?'

'What do you mean?'

There's rustling and I feel my pocket get heavier. 'I don't want your money. I've taken care of Mum by myself this long without handouts and I'm not going to start now.'

I can't say anything because she lets me go and storms away down the corridor. Matt, Ethan, and Tyler laugh so hard they're practically rolling around on the floor.

'Looks like his bodyguard has sacked him,' Matt laughs.

I don't get it—Lib needs money and I gave it to her. It's simple. But life isn't simple any more, is it? Nothing is. Everything changes. Everyone leaves me behind. No, not everyone. I have to get out of school. I have to see Gizmo. There's nothing complicated about Gizmo. He loves me no matter what.

I push past the crowds and run home. School will want to know where I went but I'll worry about that tomorrow. Right now, I just need to be at home before I have a full-blown freakout. I open the front door and run to Gizmo's bed. I bury my face in his neck and let the tears go. I know he'll give me kisses and make me feel better. He normally does, anyway. I wipe my face with the back of my sleeve. Why hasn't he moved?

'Gizmo?'

'GIZMO?'

Chapter Thirty-Three

No. No, no, no. This can't be happening. It's too soon. I'm not ready.

I tried to get Mum to take us to the vet's but she didn't answer her phone. Dad couldn't get out of work. In the end, it was Rosa who brought us. She tried to calm me down in the car, telling me how to do stupid yoga relaxation exercises, but I didn't listen. I was too focused on Gizmo's chest, watching it gently rise and fall. As long as that's happening, he's still here.

I couldn't take it in that vet's room. I sat on the floor trying to breathe but the air was like treacle. Rosa rubbed my back and made soothing sounds, but it was all noise to me. I tried to tell myself it could just be another infection but I couldn't make myself believe it.

The vet gave Gizmo an injection, then used a tube to drain fluid from his belly. He just lay there, breathing jerkily. When she'd finished, she came over and crouched in front of me and Rosa. She smiled, but it wasn't a proper smile. It was thin and her eyes were sad. 'I wish I had better news,' she said.

What she said after that blurred into nothingness. I remember snatches of phrases—'kidneys failing' was one.

I managed to croak out a question. I wanted to know if this was my fault. If me teaching him tricks did this to him. The vet said no. She said it would have happened if he'd done nothing but loll around on the sofa. It just happens with old dogs.

But there has to be something you can do.

There's nothing we can do.

Prolonging things would be cruel.

We should consider putting him to sleep.

I jumped to my feet and cried, 'I'm not going to let you kill him!' I scooped him up and carried him out to the waiting room. I saw the vet talking to Rosa in the doorway but I didn't want to hear it. I wanted to get away. Vets are supposed to make animals better, not murder them.

We're home now. Gizmo is lying on my bed, asleep. I'm holding him tight. If I hold him, he can't go anywhere. I can tether him to Earth like a weight on a balloon. I hear Mum, Dad, and Rosa talking downstairs. Sometimes their voices go loud. Mum and Dad's, anyway. Rosa is always the calm one. God, she's annoying.

'Hey, Gizmo,' I say. 'Remember that time Dad tied your lead to a bin outside a shop, but it was really light and you pulled it over? Then dragged it around the street? People were proper angry, but I thought it was brilliant. Remember, Gizmo?'

His eyelids flutter but he doesn't stir.

'Remember when you ate Mum's red lipstick? And you got it on the carpet? The stain never did come out. And your poos were pink for a week!'

I wish he'd get better—jump up, spin, yip for a treat, run to his lead. I'd even settle for a kiss. The door opens downstairs.

'George?' Mum calls from the bottom. 'Could you come down for a second?'

I pick up Gizmo and carry him downstairs, placing him carefully on his bed in the living room. Mum is perched on the edge of the chair nearest the window. Dad and Rosa are on the sofa. Dad clutches his old favourite tea mug in two hands. No one is looking at anyone. I sit on the floor next to Gizmo and stroke him.

'George,' says Mum. 'We've been having a chat. And we agree it would be best if we take Gizmo to the vet tomorrow.'

'What for?' I ask. 'A second opinion?'

Mum blinks slowly and sighs. She's about to speak when—

'What your mum is trying to say is, the humane option would be to have Gizmo . . . put to sleep.'

'I know what I'm trying to say, Rosa,' says Mum, an edge to her voice. 'I don't need your help, thank you very much.'

'Steady on,' says Dad. 'There's no need to get shirty.'

Mum scowls. 'What's she even here for, anyway? What does any of this have to do with her?'

Rosa drops her eyes to the floor and fiddles with her necklace.

'In case you were unaware, Rosa took the dog to the vet's,' says Dad. 'As you were clearly too busy.'

Mum slams her tea down. 'You're damn right I was too busy. I have to work all the hours God sends since you went off!'

I've heard enough. I pick up Gizmo and head back out but everyone calls me back.

'This kind of conflict is incredibly damaging for children,' says Rosa. 'Please, let's work together constructively.'

'Will you PLEASE shut up?' Mum snaps. 'You are not helping. Did you know we've had Gizmo since before George? He was essentially our first child and George loves him more than anything in this world. So, sorry if I'm a little upset, OK?'

It goes quiet again. I wondered when this was going to happen again. They haven't had a row like this for ages. For the last year or so it's just been tense conversations about money. It's like a storm breaking on a muggy day.

'So you're all saying you want Gizmo to die?' I say, my voice strangled.

'Oh sweetheart,' says Mum, her eyes wet. 'I'm afraid he's going to die soon anyway. At the vet's it will be painless and peaceful.'

Gizmo opens his eyes slightly before closing them again and breathing out heavily through his nose.

'It won't be all bad, son,' says Dad. 'We'll book

him in for late in the day tomorrow and give him the best last day ever; treats, the lot.'

'We know you love him, son,' says Mum. 'So you have to do the right thing for him. Let him go.'

I look at Dad and Rosa. They both nod. There's no getting around it. Tonight is going to be my last night with Gizmo.

Chapter Thirty-Four

I can't sleep. And why would I? I've done nothing but look at Gizmo. He's perked up a little. He's woken up. He can walk around a bit.

And it just makes me think, what if the vet is wrong? Miracle recoveries can happen. You hear about them all the time.

It's nearly six a.m. I get up and look out of my window. The sun is already up, but the light is weak and hazy. It reminds me of when we had to be up at about this time to get to the airport for our flight to Spain. Hugging Gizmo goodbye before we left and hoping Auntie Gloria would take good care of him.

From my window, I can see the fields way off in the distance, with the railway line running through them. On quiet nights, I can hear the trains in the distance.

Gizmo is snoozing softly on my bed. I can't give up on him so easily, and I can't believe Mum and Dad are. I think about arguing with them, but what's the point? It'll all come to nothing. They'll just end up turning on each other and nothing will change. A plan starts to form in my head. I don't want to think about it too much because I'll talk myself out of it.

I tiptoe down the stairs, sticking to the least creaky side nearest the wall. I creep into the kitchen and turn on the light. Mum has left all of Gizmo's treats out on the side. I grab a bag and sweep them into it. Then I fill up an empty squash bottle with water and drop that in. Then I pick up some snacks for me.

I go back upstairs and dress as quietly as I can by the light of my lamp. If Mum wakes up it's game over. I stuff the envelope of cash into the bag, then pick Gizmo up and carry him downstairs. He wearily kisses my chin. See? He's getting better already.

I've googled and there are no trains direct to Golden Beach from Tammerstone. You have to change like five times. The quickest way to get there is to get the bus to the city centre, and then get the coach from there to Golden Beach. The whole journey should take about four hours. The first bus doesn't leave until eight which means I'm going to have to keep a low profile around town until then. Mum is going to be up soon and I can't have her finding me. Remembering what happened with her tracking me to the big hill, I leave my phone on the side. I'm about to leave but I stop. I can't just disappear. I'll leave a note.

Mum,

Don't worry, I'm not running away for ever. I'm just not going to give up on Gizmo. He deserves a chance.

Love,
George.

With that, I pick up Gizmo and quietly leave the house.

Gizmo is more alert when we get outside, so once we're out of the street, I put him down so he can have a wee. He wobbles a little as he walks, but he's fine otherwise.

I nip into the shop on Johnson Street and buy some Jammie Dodgers. I'm going to have to pick up the pace now, Mum is going to be getting up soon and she's going to see my letter. Then she'll probably call Dad and they'll both be out looking for me. No doubt Rosa will know exactly what to do in these situations, what with her being an 'expert' and all that, so I need to have my wits about me. I decide to head to the park. There are loads of trees and bushes so there'll always be a hiding place if we need one.

I sit down at the foot of the bank and put Gizmo down. He sits up and looks around. He knows where he is. He's had so many good times here: playing fetch, jumping in the lake, eating ice cream. I can tell he wants nothing more than to jump up and take off across the grass, pick up a stick and bring it back. But he's just too tired.

The sun's out now. I can tell it's going to be a warm day. Perfect for another adventure.

The Intergalactic Power Squad Conquers the Space Rock of Zagron

We returned to the Intergalactic Power Squad base to get dry. George was annoyed to find Dad had stuck a flip-flop on the roof of the command centre.

We ate sandwiches and ice cream and I drank cold water from a tap. Afterwards, I lay in the sun and fell asleep. I could get used to being a beach dog.

When I woke up, George was fully dressed, with his Ultra Shoes on. 'Hello boy,' he said. 'Are you ready to conquer the Space Rock of Zagron?'

Dad left the beach because he'd noticed a pub was selling beer in plastic cups and he said he was feeling 'thirsty'. Mum tutted and rolled her eyes but insisted he brought back two.

'Mum,' said George. 'We're going for a walk up the beach.'

'All right, love,' she replied, turning a page in her book.

George nodded at me and we headed towards the Space Rock of Zagron. It loomed on the horizon like a real mountain.

As we walked, the beach got quieter. This end was more stony and people seemed to prefer it where the deckchairs were. By the time we reached the rock, we were the only ones around.

'OK, Wonder Dog,' said George. 'You wait here and be on the lookout for Crab People.'

I spun around and gave a little yip so he knew I understood my order. He ruffled my fur and went around the other side of the rock where it wasn't quite so steep. I could hear him scrambling up, getting footholds in the natural shelves of the rock. I heard him gasp a little. I think he caught his knee on a sharp edge.

The Space Rock of Zagron was a bit of a weird shape. It had tall sides but a big dip in the middle. Kind of like a giant, uneven doughnut. The tallest side was the one I was watching. I heard him skid down into the dip.

'I'm in the crater, Wonder Dog,' he yelled. 'No Crab People present, but I will remain vigig . . . vigigil . . . I'll keep my eyes open.'

I heard him scrambling to get up the tallest side; the one closest to me. He grunted and groaned as he tried to pull himself up. It seemed to take for ever. Eventually, I saw his head poke up at the top. He was pink-faced and sweaty. He pulled himself up and put his knee on the ledge, then his other knee. Slowly, he stood up on top of the rock.

I barked in celebration and George threw his arms in the air. 'I did it, boy! I claim the Space Rock of Zagron in the name of the Intergalactic Power Sq—'

His arms went down and started waving. His feet slipped from under him. There was a bang. He disappeared.

Where are you, Ultra Boy?

Chapter Thirty-Five

It's ten to eight and I'm at the bus stop. Well, I'm actually behind the bus stop. I feel too exposed standing there facing the road. Gizmo is on the floor, sniffing at a patch of grass. Loads of kids are walking past on their way to school. I keep my head down and don't make eye contact. I don't need anyone bothering me. Ten minutes until the bus gets here.

'Is that you, freakshow?'

I close my eyes and sigh.

'It is,' says Matt, flanked as ever by Ethan and Tyler. 'Man, your old mum is worried about you. She called my mum earlier, all, "Ooooh, is our George with you? I know they spend a lot of time together".' Matt laughs. 'Looks like you haven't been keeping her up to date. I'd rather spend my time with your knackered old dog than you. At least he doesn't lose his mind with panic all the time.' He pretends to struggle for breath and flaps his hands in front of his face. 'Ooh, I fell over once. Send me to the loony bin!'

I wind Gizmo's lead around my fist and clench it tight. Seven minutes until the bus gets here.

'Why don't you ever speak, freakshow?' says Ethan. 'Would it help if we barked?'

Matt steps closer. Looking at him, I can't believe it's the same person I had so many good times with. How can a person change so much?

'Easy lads,' says Matt. 'Georgie Boy's probably upset because he's got to kill his dog today.'

Matt jerks backwards. What have I done? I look down at my clenched fist, shaking. Did I just try to hit him? I'm pretty sure I skimmed the end of his nose. His face slackens, his eyes go wide, his mouth drops open. For a second, I see the old Matt. The kid that would never say no to an adventure. The kid who would have been standing with me, not against. He touches the end of his nose. It has gone red.

'You know what I'm going to do?' he says, snarling at me.

'Don't know. Guide Santa's sleigh?'

He growls under his breath. 'Get him.'

I scoop up Gizmo and run away. Tyler and Ethan are close behind. I sprint across the road and through the alley back into the park. I turn left and cut through the trees. If I can make it through there I'll be able to get to the shops. They can't beat me up in a shop. Can they? I hope Gizmo is OK. Being bounced around can't be good for him. I'm halfway through the woods when a shape drops in front of me. Ethan. He must have cut through a garden and hopped a wall. I try to get around him but he makes himself huge like a bear and stops me with his arm. Matt and Tyler arrive behind me. We're surrounded.

'Put the dog down,' says Matt.

I shake my head.

'Either put him down or the lads will drag him off you,' he says.

I look around for signs of anyone who might save me, but the woods are deserted as usual. I slowly put Gizmo down behind me.

'Now put your bag down.'

I do as I'm told. My mind is buzzing with ideas to try and escape but there are too many to keep track of. It's like when you see an air traffic control radar on telly, tiny dots flying all over the place.

Tyler crouches and opens my bag, digging through it and throwing everything out—Gizmo's treats, food, drinks.

'You don't lay hands on me and get away with it, freakshow,' says Matt.

'You won't find anything useful in there,' I say to Tyler, ignoring Matt. 'Just a load of dog stuff.'

Tyler doesn't listen and carries on digging. When he finds nothing in the main part of the bag, he goes for the front zip. I try to stop him but Ethan holds me back.

'Must be something juicy in there, boys,' says Matt, rubbing his hands together like a cartoon villain.

I know there's no way he won't find it, and sure enough, five seconds later the cash-stuffed envelope is in Tyler's sausage hands. When he sees what's inside, his eyes go round like dinner plates.

'Look at this,' he says, standing up and showing the others.

'Silly boy,' says Matt. 'Walking around with this much money. What if you were to lose it?'

'Give it back,' I growl, trying to push down the waves

of sickness in my stomach.

'Or what?' says Ethan.

'Or I'll call the police,' I say.

They laugh. 'And have to explain why you're bunking off school?' says Matt. 'I don't think so.'

'Besides,' says Tyler, pressing his chest into my face. 'You know what happens to grasses.'

I step back and try to breathe. This cannot be happening. I have to do something. Here goes nothing.

'Gizmo, kill!'

I turn around and he's lying down, about to fall asleep. They all laugh again, even harder this time. I don't know why I thought he'd suddenly be able to do that. He couldn't even manage it when he was completely healthy.

'Oh no! I'm dead!' Matt whimpers. 'The dying dog finished me off.'

'See you around, freakshow,' Ethan sneers as they turn to walk away, taking my money with them. I can't let them get away with this. I pick up Gizmo and go after them, but they laugh and ignore me, counting my money.

'Give me my money back,' I beg. 'Please.'

They mimic me in an old lady voice as we leave

the woods and go into the main part of the park.

'Give me my money back.'

'How about no?'

I grab Matt's shoulder and spin him around. Tyler goes to do something, but Matt puts his hand up.

'This isn't you, Matt,' I say. 'You've changed, yeah, but not that much. Not enough to do this.'

A freakout is bubbling in my belly but it's like there's a stopper keeping it down. I hope it'll hold. I straighten my back and tilt my chin upwards, just like Lib taught me. Matt seems to step back a little and I look into his eyes in a way that normally makes me uncomfortable. I know my old friend is in there somewhere. He hasn't completely hardened, not yet. He clenches his jaw and nods, then drops the envelope on the floor.

'What are you doing?' Ethan yells. He goes to pick it up, but Matt stops him.

'Leave it, yeah?'

'Are you serious?'

'He's not worth the trouble,' he says, glancing at me over his shoulder. 'I don't want to do jail time for him.'

They seem to realize he has a point, then turn and

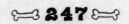

walk away. I pick up the envelope and stuff it in my pocket, then go back to Gizmo. I'm shaking.

When we get back to the stop, the bus is pulling away. I wave at the driver, but it carries on. Damn. The next one isn't for an hour.

I put Gizmo down and lean against the bus stop. I close my eyes and try to picture Golden Beach; how it's there, waiting for us to arrive.

'All right?'

I open my eyes.

'Oh,' I say. 'Hello.'

'Little man doesn't look too good,' says Lib. She kneels next to Gizmo and scratches behind his ear. I decide to tell her about what the vet said and what I'm trying to do. She stands up.

'I get it,' she says. 'You want to complete the list.'

I nod. Lib sighs and digs her hands into her pockets. 'Sorry about going off on you. Again. You were just trying to do a nice thing.'

'That's OK,' I say. 'I guess I didn't think it through enough.'

Lib smiles and sticks her hand out. I take it and she pulls me in for a crushing hug. Why do I feel like I'm going to cry? Seriously. There's a lump in my throat the size of a melon. When she lets me go, I see her eyes are watery too.

'What are you getting upset for, you massive wimp?' Lib says with a chuckle, aiming a light punch at my arm.

'Am not,' I croak. 'You are.'

Lib sniffs heavily. 'Don't confuse my hay fever with me having human emotions, Georgie Boy.'

Gizmo gently paws at Lib's foot, so she picks him up and kisses his head. 'Look,' she says, 'there's literally no point in me going to school today. I won't get any work done because I'll be too busy worrying about you two. How about we get Gizmo to the seaside?'

Disaster at the Space Rock

I couldn't hear him any more. It was quiet. I barked and barked but he didn't say anything. I ran around the rock but there was no way for me to get to him. How could he fall like that? The edge must have been slippery. I kept barking, expecting to see him climbing back over the rock, but he didn't.

I couldn't let anything bad happen to Ultra Boy. That's not Wonder Dog's style. I ran back along the beach, barking and yipping, trying to attract attention. I've never run quicker. I got back to Mum and Dad and barked at them, frantically spinning around. They were both in their deckchairs, sipping from their plastic cups.

'Quiet, Gizmo,' said Dad. 'Do you want to get us kicked off the beach?'

He must have thought George was following me. I ran over and jumped on his legs, digging my claws in.

'Hey, what do you think you're doing?' he yelled, but this time he looked up. 'Hang about, where's George?'

I barked again and ran back across the beach to

the Space Rock of Zagron, making sure they were following me. When I got back to the rock I put my front paws on it and looked up at the top, barking as loud as I could.

'George?' Mum yelled. 'Where are you?'

Chapter Thirty-Six

'So have you been to Golden Beach before?' I ask Lib.

She shakes her head. 'Only ever been to Blackpool, mate. Young carers' trip. Proper miserable. Rained all day.'

I blush a little. Hearing about Lib's life makes me realize how lucky I am in some ways. In loads of ways, actually.

'So . . . your mum,' I say. 'She'll be OK, won't she?'

Lib pops some gum in her mouth and offers me one. I take it and my mouth explodes with mintiness.

'She has a woman that comes in a couple of times a week,' says Lib. 'She'll help her wash, give her something to eat and that. As long as I'm back by tonight, everything will be fine.'

I take a breath. The gum is so strong, it's kind of burning my nose. 'So, if you don't mind me asking . . .' I start the question but don't know how to finish it.

'MS,' says Lib. 'She has good days and bad days.'

Oh, I've heard about MS. One of Mum's friends has it. She used to run marathons but now she can hardly walk to the end of her road without becoming exhausted. It sounds horrible.

'I'm really sorry to hear that,' I say.

Lib nods. 'Yeah, cheers. Is what it is.'

I've never been sure what that means so I don't say anything. I guess it's just a way of accepting stuff you can't change. I should probably be more like that sometimes.

I hear a car approaching at the top of the road. The way the engine squeals and clunks sounds familiar. Oh no. Oh no! I grab Gizmo and scramble behind a bush at the end of someone's garden. I hope they're not in.

'Oh, is that you, Lib?' I recognize Mum's voice.

'Yeah, hi,' says Lib.

'Oh my God, we're worried sick. Have you seen George anywhere?' says Mum.

My stomach twists with guilt and I screw my eyes

shut to try and stop the tears.

'Sorry,' says Lib. 'Is he missing, then?'

'How come you're not in school, anyway?' I hear Dad's panicked voice.

'Free period,' says Lib. And then, 'Hey. How you doing, Rosa? They got you on the case?'

Hang on. How does she know Rosa?

'I am not here in a professional capacity,' says Rosa.

'For God's sake, who cares?' says Mum, exasperated. 'Look, if you see him get in touch. Here's my number, OK?'

'Yeah, I will. Thanks,' says Lib.

Footsteps hurry back into the car. As it pulls off, I step back around to where I was.

'You all right?' says Lib, slugging me on the shoulder.

I sniffle a bit and scratch behind Gizmo's ear. 'Fine.'

I've got to stop feeling bad. If I go back, they'll take Gizmo to the vet's and they'll strap him down and kill him. There's no way I can let that happen. When I get to Golden Beach, I'll let them know I'm safe.

'How do you know Rosa?' I ask.

'She's been round my flat a few times,' says Lib. 'She's not bad, it's the system that's screwed, you know? Tell you what though, with her on the case, things are going to be more difficult.'

'What do you mean?'

'She's used to runaways,' says Lib. 'She'll know how to track you down. Trust me, I know.'

'What do you mean?' I ask.

'Never mind.' Lib shakes her head quick. 'Bussing it is going to be too risky. Train too. They'll have called the cops, and knowing Rosa, the bus and train companies as well.'

'So what do you suggest?'

Lib narrows her eyes and runs her tongue across her top teeth. 'We could get a taxi.'

'Taxi?' I say. 'Won't that cost loads?'

'Probably,' says Lib. 'No more than four hundred quid, though.'

It's worth a go, I suppose.

'Right, taxi rank is just up the road,' says Lib. 'Put your hood up and keep your head down.'

We round the corner and see a line of taxis. Beer-bellied drivers stand outside their cars, chatting. I hope at least one of them fancies a long journey. We're just about to approach one when a loud burst of static cuts through the hubbub.

'Calling all drivers, calling all drivers.'

'Eh up!' one of them chuckles, folding his newspaper in half. 'This must be good.'

'We've just had a call from a social worker. Be on the lookout for a boy by the name of George. Thirteen years old, will have an elderly dog with him.'

'Keep walking,' Lib mutters under her breath. 'Go, go, go.'

What are we supposed to do now? We're never going to get there! No, we can't give up. Gizmo has to get on that beach before … before …

CRASH! A bolt of lightning, sent from God's own finger, bounces off the ground in front of me. Well, not really, but it might as well have. A blue van, with its back doors open, and cracked white lettering on the side saying, 'ANGLIA POWDER COATINGS—ROMBURY.'

'What's the matter, George?' says Lib.

I point at the van parked in front of us. 'Rombury is just down the road from Golden Beach,' I say. 'Literally a few miles away. Maybe we should ask them for a lift.'

Lib shakes her head. 'Too risky. They'd want to

know why we're off school and might smell a rat.' She peers into the van. There is a big sheet of blue tarpaulin in there, right behind the cab. 'We'll have to hide in here.'

I look into the van, then at Gizmo. I'll do whatever it takes to get him to Golden Beach.

'Are you sure you want to do this?' I whisper to Lib.

'I've been with you this far, I might as well see it through,' she says. 'Right boys. Let's go.'

Alone

Everything that happened after that was confusing. Dad scrambled over the side and looked down. All I could hear him say was, 'Oh no, oh no, oh no.' He slid down into the dip while Mum screamed at him, asking what was wrong. He didn't answer so she went after him and climbed up herself.

They called his name but he didn't answer. They slowly brought him out and laid him on the sand. His eyes were closed and the yellow sand turned red underneath his head. Dad took off his shirt and put George's head on it. I tried to get close to give him a kiss, but Mum was too frantic. Soon, men and women in green shirts arrived and put a mask on George. They strapped him to a bed and put it in the back of a big van with flashing lights. Mum got in with him while Dad took me back to the chalet then left in his car.

I sat by the door and waited. George would be back any minute, I just knew it.

Some time later, the door did open, but it wasn't George. It was Dad. He rushed straight past me and into our bedroom, where he stuffed some things into a bag. He moved all around the chalet, mumbling to himself. I followed closely behind him, trying to understand what had happened to George. But Dad wasn't there, not really. His mind was in another place. He refilled my water bowl and gave me some food. That was when he really noticed me. He ruffled my fur and planted a big kiss on my head, which was unusual for him, because he never normally did that.

'Thank you so much, Gizmo,' he said. 'You're a good boy.'

With that, he turned and left again.

Chapter Thirty-Seven

So this is an adventure, all right. I mean, I'm slightly concerned about how we're going to get out once we're there, but I'm sure it'll be fine. It has to be. I've never been a big believer in signs and things like that, but this van being here has to be one.

Luckily, the tarpaulin is big enough for all three of us to hide under and we settle as best we can without making too much noise. Once we're away, we'll be able to come out of hiding. Gizmo is already looking sleepy so I take off my hoody and make a little bed for him.

The engine starts up and we pull away. This is really happening. We're actually doing it. I lower the sheet and take a few deep breaths away from the hot plastic. The van screeches to a stop. What's happening? Do they know we're here? We quickly hide again. I bury my face in Gizmo's fur. I hear hurried footsteps. Muffled banging and shouting. The back doors flying open.

THUNK. Something heavy is dropped into the van, then the doors slam. In a few seconds, it pulls away again. I'm thrown against the wall by the sheer force. Gizmo starts to slide but Lib manages to grab him before he gets hurt.

'What's going on?' I mouth to Lib.

We peek over the tarp and see a black holdall by the back doors.

Lib shakes her head then goes to crawl out from our hiding place, but the speed of the van throws her back. She gets to her feet and crouch-walks to the back doors, gripping the walls as she goes. I grab Gizmo and hold him close. In a couple of seconds, Lib stumbles back with the holdall. Grabbing a cable on the wall to steady herself, she unzips it. When I see what's inside, I gasp. There must be tens of thousands of pounds in there.

This isn't just a normal van—it's a getaway vehicle.

After the Space Rock

'Gizmo!' I'm woken up by a massive hug. I open
my eyes and there is George. He has a big bandage
around his head and he's all bruised. Mum and Dad
tell him to calm down, but he's too pleased to see me.
I jump up and kiss his hurt face.

'You saved me, boy!' he said. 'You're a hero!'

I don't know what he means. I was just doing my
job. He had been away from me for two days. They
felt like a lifetime.

Mum and Dad look tired and grey. At the
beginning of the holiday, they had laughed and held
each other's hands. Now they stood apart and looked
at each other with anger.

On the car journey home, shouting erupted. It
was so loud, it hurt my ears. I heard Mum say, 'If
you hadn't gone for your poxy beer, it wouldn't have
happened.' Dad laughed, but it wasn't the fun laugh
I was used to. It was as rough and hard as the Space
Rock of Zagron. 'Says the person who couldn't put
her book down for two minutes to watch her son.
Some mother you are.'

The car screeched to a halt. 'Get out,' she said.

'What are you talking about? It's another fifty miles home,' said Dad.

'Then you'll walk,' she said. 'Out.'

He got out.

Chapter Thirty-Eight

'What are we going to do? What are we going to do? What are we going to do?'

Lib makes a 'quieten down' gesture and glares daggers at me. 'The first thing we're going to do is keep calm,' she whispers. 'Can you call the police?'

'No! I left my phone at home,' I yelp. 'Can you?'

Lib screws her eyes shut. 'I had to sell my phone.'

Oh no. Oh no.

Lib opens her eyes and grabs my shoulders like she can sense I'm about to have a freakout. 'Listen, we're going to sit tight until they stop. Who says they're going to check under here? When they're clear, we'll make a run for it.'

I take deep breaths and try to imagine a flat,

glassy ocean. Then the van screeches around a corner and I nearly brain myself on the handle sticking out of the wall.

I check on Gizmo but he's sleeping through everything. I can't believe this is happening. Only I could turn a trip to the seaside into being an accessory to a heist.

'I wonder how much is in there,' Lib whispers, nodding at the bag.

I shrug.

'You know, when we escape and turn these guys in, we might get a reward,' she says.

I can't think that far ahead right now. I'm just focusing on running as fast as I can when I need to. I'll have to carry Gizmo and hope he doesn't get too distressed.

Time seems to slow down. I have no way of knowing how much has passed. It's like being sealed in a box outside of the real world. We might have been sitting here for twenty minutes or twenty hours.

After a while, Gizmo wakes up. He yawns and softly blinks. He hasn't eaten in ages. I grab some Meaty Schmackos out of my bag and he greedily gobbles them down. Wow, there's nothing wrong with his appetite. I give him another, which he eats just as quickly.

I don't know how long we've been driving when the van stops. What's going on? Are we there? Footsteps around the side of the van. We lie down flat and make sure we're completely covered. The doors open. It sounds like two people are climbing into the back.

'What have we got, then?'

'Pretty good haul this time.'

'Must be a hundred thousand here, easy.'

It's a man and a woman, that's all I can tell. I feel Lib shift. What's she doing? She can't be thinking of jumping out at them, can she? What if they have guns? I slowly reach out and grip her ankle, which is near my head. We'll stay put and hope they don't find us. As long as we stay perfectly—

PRRRRRFFFT.

'Was that you?' the woman says.

'No, I thought it was you.'

Oh no. Oh no, oh no, oh no. Gizmo has, to put it in my Dad's terms, 'dropped his guts'. Ugh, this might be the worst fart he has ever done, and being stuck under this sheet is making it a million times worse. It must be those Meaty Schmackos. It's been so long since he's had them, his stomach probably isn't used to them.

'Oh, I think I'm going to be sick,' the woman groans. 'You're such a dirty old man, Graham.'

'It wasn't me!'

PLLLLLLLLLLLLLFRRRRAP!

'You're doing it again! What's the matter with you?'

I grip Gizmo hard, as if that will somehow stop him doing another one, but of course, it has the opposite effect.

RRRRRRRRAMMPAMPAMPAMPAM.

Silence. I hold my breath.

'It's coming from over there,' says the man.

'Stop making excuses, Graham.'

'It's definitely coming from over there. I can't throw my farts.'

What do we do? What do we do? What do we do?

The sheet is pulled away and two dark figures loom over us. 'What the hell are you doing in here?'

Chapter Thirty-Nine

'What's the matter with him? Is he having an asthma attack or something?'

'It's a panic attack,' says Lib. 'Stand back and give him some space.'

I'm trying to breathe but it's like I'm submerged in a swamp and the air is thick and grimy. I stare at a patch of fur on the back of Gizmo's neck. I reduce the entire world, the entire universe, to that patch of fur. Those two people all dressed in black aren't there. It's just the fur. My breathing begins to slow. I wipe the tears from my cheeks but never take my eyes from it.

'No, we won't give him some space,' says the woman. 'Until you explain what you're doing in our van.'

'We wanted to get to Golden Beach,' I whisper. 'And we saw you had Rombury on the van.'

The woman grunts and smacks the man on the shoulder. 'I told you this van was a bad idea.'

'Sorry, Mandy,' says the man, which earns him another smack.

'Don't use my name in front of them, you cretin.'

'They've already seen our faces,' says Graham. 'What difference does it make?'

The woman narrows her icy blue eyes and stares at us.

'Just let us go, yeah?' says Lib. 'We won't grass.'

'You must think I came down with the last shower,' says Mandy. 'Up.'

Lib and I look at each other. What are we supposed to do?

'I said up!' Mandy screeches.

We do as she tells us. 'Come on, we're going in the warehouse,' she says.

'What if we don't want to?' says Lib.

The man, who looks like he should wrestle for WWE, reaches behind him and pulls out a baseball bat.

'Any more questions?'

The man grabs Lib by the arm and shoves her

towards the door. I follow with Gizmo. The van is backed up to an open warehouse loading bay.

It's dingy inside with some fading strip lighting the only thing keeping it from darkness.

'So what we doing with them?' the big man asks.

Mandy smirks. 'I reckon we can make today an even bigger earner. You got families?'

Neither of us answers.

'Course you have,' she goes on. 'And I bet they'll be really keen to have you home. So keen they'll pay what we want.'

'Ransom, are you serious?' I say. 'My parents don't have any money!'

'I'm sure they'll find it from somewhere,' she says.

Mandy steps closer to me and glares at Gizmo. 'I don't reckon the dog's going to be much use, though.'

'What's that supposed to mean?'

'Put it down.'

'No,' I say, clutching Gizmo closer.

Graham points the bat at me, his face cold and expressionless. I gently put Gizmo on the ground.

'That mutt looks pretty old,' says Mandy. 'Best to put it out of its misery.'

'Don't you dare,' says Lib.

'Go on, then,' says Mandy to Graham.

Graham pulls back the bat, his piggy eyes on Gizmo. No! They can't! I leap in front of him, and he stops just before it hits me.

'Are you stupid or something?' he booms.

'Never mind, hit him instead!' Mandy orders.

Graham taps the end of the bat on the concrete floor then pulls it back. I screw my eyes shut. This is going to hurt.

'AAAAARRRGGHHH!'

I open my eyes and Gizmo has his teeth clamped around Graham. In an area you REALLY don't want dog teeth to be clamped.

'Getitoffme getitoffme getitoffme.'

Mandy tries to prise Gizmo off him, but all she gets is a bite to the hand for her trouble. Graham drops the bat and hits the ground, howling. I pick up the bat as Mandy shakes off Gizmo and lunges at Lib, who goes low and shoulder charges her to the floor. Graham makes a grab for me but I swing the bat and he backs off.

'Ready?' Lib breathes. 'Now.'

I scoop up Gizmo and we turn and sprint for the exit. Lib gets out ahead of us, and just as I'm about to squeeze through the gap between the van and the edge of the door, I see a big green button. I mash it with my palm and jump through. The door slides down and closes just as Mandy and Graham get to it.

Outside, Lib finds an empty beer bottle and smashes the end on the edge of a wall.

'What are you doing?' I yell.

Lib ignores me and uses the jagged edge to slash all the tyres on the van. 'Just making sure they don't go anywhere.'

The door starts to open behind us so we sprint out of the yard and find ourselves in the middle of a half-abandoned industrial estate. We keep running, knowing they could be after us at any moment. On one side there's a long stretch of derelict warehouses and on the other side, a load of scrubland, all five-foot stingers and strips of plastic sheeting.

We turn the corner and see a cabin with a faded 'Deb's Diner' sign on it. We hurtle inside and find a woman, who I'm guessing is Deb, wiping the counter down. She looks at us like we've just landed in a flying saucer. I suppose she doesn't get too many kids in here. Or dogs.

'Can I help you?' she asks, still frowning.

'We need to use your phone,' I say, panting.

Deb's eyes narrow and she folds her arms. 'Is this some kind of scam?'

'No!' says Lib. 'We've got to call the police. Two people in a warehouse down there have stolen loads of money.'

Deb still doesn't move. 'How do I know you're not just going to run off with my phone?'

'Fine, you call them,' I yell. 'Just do it now before they get away!'

'All right, keep your hair on,' she says, dialling 999.

I move a moth-eaten net curtain out of the way and look out of the window. You can just about see the warehouse from here.

'Yeah, I'd like to report a theft . . . Loads of

money, apparently. Bertram Industrial Estate, Rombury.'

'Tell them there are two dangerous people on site,' I say. 'And hurry!'

We stay in the cafe until we hear the sirens coming down the street. Then we go out and watch from the other side of the street as Mandy and Graham are bundled out in handcuffs.

'Two more bad guys put away,' I say, quoting my comic. 'And it's all thanks to Gizmo the Wonder Dog.'

Lib laughs and gives Gizmo a kiss. 'Good work, boy. Right, let's get back to Deb's and call a taxi to Golden Beach.'

I know she's right. We can't stay and give a statement because they'd find out I'm missing and they wouldn't let us go. We can talk to the police later.

HAVE ONE MORE ULTRA BOY
AND WONDER DOG ADVENTURE ✓

Golden Beach: The Aftermath

Golden Beach was where everything changed. We arrived as one family and left as another.

The arguments between Mum and Dad would sometimes stop for ages, but when they started again, they always went back to that day.

One day, a few months later, we were having a barbeque in the garden, and Mum had forgotten to buy a certain kind of meat. Dad snapped about it and she snapped right back. Soon, we were back on Golden Beach, the two of them blaming each other for what had happened. George went to get up and leave but he fell back down in the chair, breathless. He didn't know what was happening. No one did. It was his first freakout.

People thought he was traumatized by the fall but it wasn't just that. He told me so at night when we were huddled under the covers. It was because he blamed himself for ruining the family. If he hadn't been stupid and climbed that rock, everything would still have been good.

I tried to help him as much as I could but nothing stopped him believing that. Maybe nothing ever will.

Chapter Forty

Golden Beach is smaller than I remember. In my memory, the pier stretched way out into the ocean and the rollercoaster at the fair was like something from Disneyland. In reality, the pier stops before the water is waist-height and the rollercoaster is a caterpillar. But the smells are the same, and they flow in like honey through the open taxi window. Tangy sea air, hot dogs, onions, candyfloss. The sounds too—the greedy seagulls, the loud teddy-grabber machines, the bearded old man bellowing, 'Have a boat ride by the seaside.'

Gizmo is more alert now; his ears are up, his nose is twitching. I know he knows where we are. The taxi driver lets us out by a pale-pink B & B and I pay him forty pounds.

'You hungry?' I say to Lib, nodding at the chippy next door.

'Starving,' she says.

I leave Gizmo with Lib and buy two large portions of fish and chips and a saveloy for Gizmo. Saveloys are his favourite. We cross the road and take the stone stairs down to the beach. The sand is wet and strewn with dark-purple seaweed. I put Gizmo down and let him trot next to us while we tear into our chips. I deliberately don't turn my head to the right. I don't want to see the Space Rock of Zagron yet. After what we've been through this morning, this all feels so beautifully normal. I almost forget I'm a missing person. A police car rolls down the front and I turn towards the sea so they can't see my face.

I tear off a piece of fish and shove it in my mouth. I'm so ready for this, and my God, this is the best fish I have ever had. The golden batter is light and fluffy, but crunchy too. I could eat eight of these things.

'There's a party in my mouth,' Lib moans.

Gizmo skips ahead a bit and disappears around the back of a pile of black rocks, then reappears with a long stick. He slowly brings it over to us and drops it at my feet. I know he's not going to be able to go far so I lightly chuck it towards the sea. Gizmo wags his tail and walks over to it. He picks it up and turns to come back, but his legs buckle and he falls over. Lib takes my chips for me and I run and pick him up. He gives me a kiss, then his nose starts twitching in the direction of the saveloy Lib's holding. Nothing wrong with his sense of smell. Lib tears a third off and gives it to him and he gobbles it down in about half a second. Nothing wrong with his appetite, either. Lib scratches behind Gizmo's ear then gives him the rest, which disappears just as quick.

We keep walking until we arrive at an ice cream van. You know what? I don't think this is just any old ice cream van. This is *the* ice cream van—the same one from last time! I remember it. *Albertelli's Italian Ices*. We finish our fish and chips and I buy Gizmo a ninety-nine—the full works. I'm talking a Flake, raspberry sauce, hundreds and thousands. We sit on the sand, pretty much where we sat with Mum and Dad, and I hold it up for Gizmo. He gratefully licks at it, coating his nose and muzzle with ice cream.

Lib sighs. 'I'm glad we made it.'

'Me too,' I say.

VISIT GOLDEN BEACH ✓
HAVE AN ICE CREAM ✓

Chapter Forty-One

I carefully put Gizmo down in the surf. He paws
at the water, that Gizmo smile on his face. I know
he'd like to swim, but paddling will have to do. He's
always loved the water. Except at bath time. For
some reason, that was the worst thing in the world.
But the sea, lakes, rivers, paddling pools? You could
never keep him away.

The sun is peeking out from behind the clouds,
making light dance on the waves as they splash
on his fur. This has to be better than being sent to
the vet's and strapped to a bed, and . . . Even with
everything that's happened, I'm pleased we're here.

Gizmo shakes himself a little and yips at
something in the distance. I turn around and see
what he's looking at.

'That's just a pile of rocks, boy,' I say.

He starts walking towards it, which is when I realize that the pile of rocks is none other than the Space Rock of Zagron. But the Space Rock was massive. This is nothing. What happened? The closer we get, the clearer it becomes. This *is* the real Space Rock of Zagron. Man. It's like going inside a dragon's lair and finding a leopard gecko. I suppose I built it up in my mind for so long, I exaggerated it. It doesn't seem as scary any more. Gizmo slowly walks over to it and barks a little more.

'What's this?' Lib asks.

'It's a long story,' I reply. 'Actually,' I go into my bag and pull out my notepad, 'I've kind of written it down. We both have. It's sort of Gizmo's autobiography.'

Gizmo paws my leg and I pick him up.

'I know you like reading, so . . .'

Lib nods. 'Thanks mate. This is brilliant.'

We settle on the sea wall while I dry Gizmo. I wrap him in the towel, leaving just his face poking out and put him on my lap, looking out at the sea. I hold him gently as he falls asleep. I get Mr Monkey out of the bag and put it next to him. He never sleeps without Mr Monkey.

 **280**

We don't speak; Lib is too busy reading Gizmo's autobiography anyway. I just watch the waves lap on the shore as the late-afternoon sun thinks about setting. A couple of young kids run past with their kite while their Mum and Dad look on. I want to tell them to make the most of it. All that could end at any time. It reminds me of something Dr Kaur used to say to me: live in the moment. Tell yourself that right now, everything is fine. Right now, everything is fine. Right now, everything is—

'Oh my God, George!'

Fine?

Chapter Forty-Two

Hands grab me and hold me close. Kisses pepper my face.

'Don't you ever do that again, you silly boy!'

Mum's face fills my field of vision. She's crying and her eyes are pink and puffy. I feel horrible. When she moves back a little, Dad and Rosa are there, too. Dad scowls at Lib.

'What do you think you're doing, kidnapping my son? I'm going to have you arrested.'

'Stop it, Dad,' I say. 'She didn't kidnap me. She's saved me today. Lots of times.'

'What do you mean, saved you?' says Mum. 'What happened?'

I sigh. 'I don't want to talk about it now. I've

come here to have a nice day with Gizmo, and that's what I'm going to do.'

'No, you are not, you're coming home right now,' says Dad, grabbing my arm.

'Get your hands off him!' Mum yells so loud, everyone in the area stops and looks.

'Please, everyone,' says Rosa. 'This kind of acrimony helps no one. Why don't we all just stop for a second and take a deep breath?'

'Oh, do shut up,' says Mum.

'No,' I say. 'Rosa's right.' I glance up and see she's blushing a little. And I realize this is probably the first time I've ever said anything nice about her. 'Everyone needs to calm down. Don't you remember what it was like the last time we were here? Gizmo was skipping around, you two weren't arguing, Matt was still my friend. I didn't have a single thing to worry about. I can barely remember what that's like.'

Mum and Dad look at each other for a split second, but I notice it.

'And I know that things change and life moves on, and that we're not a mosquito in amber.' Lib smiles and claps me on the shoulder. 'But I thought this might be like, I don't know, visiting a museum. Looking back at something and trying to remember what it was like.'

They all go quiet until all I can hear is the waves and the distant laughter of the kite family further down the bay.

Mum sits next to me on the wall. Dad goes to sit next to her, but then stops and kisses my forehead. 'Love you, son,' he whispers. 'I'm sorry.'

He takes a seat next to Mum. Rosa quietly sits next to Lib.

The sun is beginning to set over the ocean. The colours are amazing. I see orange, red, purple, yellow, all rippling and rolling. I've never looked at a sunset before, not really. I suppose I took them for granted, knowing I could always catch it tomorrow night, or the night after, or the night after that. This makes up for all the ones I missed, though. With every second that passes, it changes. I feel the tension of the day leave me, flowing out of my nose and mouth and disappearing into the air like smoke.

I gently touch Gizmo's head. 'What a show, eh, Gizmo?'

'Gizmo?'

Chapter Forty-Three

It's the third day of my life I've lived without Gizmo. I haven't left the house since we got back. But I don't want to be here. The house is too empty. His bed is still in my room. His lead still hangs on the Gizmo hook in the kitchen. His toys sit in the box, never to be chewed again. I can still smell him.

I've tried to finish his autobiography, but when I try I just end up getting frustrated because no matter how good I write or draw, nothing will ever recreate Gizmo. He wasn't just words, or pictures on a page. He was everything.

Gizmo came home today. In a box. It's the same size as a tub of butter. There's a plaque on top with his name on. I put it on my chest of drawers. Then

I picked up Mr Monkey and put him next to it. Gizmo could never sleep without Mr Monkey.

'Goodnight, boy,' I said. 'You saved my life in more ways than you'll ever know.'

Things have started to calm down again today. The past couple of days have been hectic. The police found out we'd been at the warehouse and came over to speak to me. They'd already talked to Lib and got the full story, but they needed me to back her up. They seized loads of evidence at the site, and Mandy and Graham will be going away for a long time. Apparently, they move around the country doing all kinds of different cons and robberies.

Word of what happened must have leaked out because soon there were reporters at the door. Mum came up and asked if I wanted her to tell them to go away, but I said no. I want the world to know how great Gizmo was.

Plucky Dog Brings Down Thieves

Police were amazed yesterday when the perpetrators of a slew of heists across the country were brought down by an elderly canine.

Gizmo's owner George Duggan, 13, and his friend Elizabeth Manzano, 15, were captured by Mandy and Graham Robinson as they staged a dramatic robbery at T.S. Crispin's Antiques Shop in Tammerstone.

Young Elizabeth says Gizmo bit the assailants, which allowed the trio to make their escape and call the police. 'We've never seen anything like it,' Detective Constable Alan Whitfield said. 'We've been tracking this pair for months and they end up getting caught by a couple of kids and a dog.'

Sadly, Gizmo, approximately 78 in dog years, passed away peacefully later that day from natural causes, but his family should take comfort in the fact that he died a hero.

Mum cut all his mentions out of the papers and collected them for me. I've pinned them to the board in my room, next to an old photo of the two of us dressed as Ultra Boy and Wonder Dog.

HAVE FIFTEEN MINUTES OF FAME

It's a shame we couldn't tick off this last thing on the list until after he died, but at least everyone got to know how amazing he is. Was.

My door opens and Mum peeps her head around, saying, 'Knock, knock.'

'You could just actually knock,' I say.

Mum rolls her eyes. 'You've got a visitor.'

I try and tell her I don't want any visitors, but it's too late. Lib is already standing in my room. She's wearing her school uniform, which tells me it must be a weekday. I've completely lost track.

'Come on, Georgie Boy, let's be having you,' she says. 'We've got places to be.'

I slump back down on my bed. 'I don't want to go anywhere.'

I see Mum raise her eyebrows at Lib and give her one of those thin-lipped smiles before she leaves. Lib sits next to me and puts her arm around me. 'Do you really think Gizmo would want you to mope around for the rest of your life?'

I shrug and stare at a stain on my carpet which I think was from when Gizmo puked. Or when I puked. I'm not sure.

'Of course he wouldn't,' Lib goes on, answering her own question. 'Now seriously, let's go. I promise you, it'll be worth it.'

I sigh. Maybe getting some fresh air would be a good idea. I pull my shoes on and we head downstairs.

'George, where are you going?' Mum calls after me.

'Just out,' I say.

She stands in front of us, hugging herself, her eyes crinkled with worry.

'I'll be back soon.'

'I promise he's not doing a runner this time,' says Lib. 'I'll make sure of that.'

Mum smiles a little and kisses me on the cheek. 'Bye, love.'

We go outside. The breeze feels harsh on my skin because I've spent so long indoors. Reginald sits on his windowsill, his head bowed as if he can tell what's happened.

'So where are we going?' I ask, glancing at the lamp post Gizmo always loved to pee on.

'It's a surprise,' says Lib.

We walk quietly through the park and along Bramcote Lane. We head past the church and onto the little lane with all the nice shops on it. We stop outside one of them.

'Look,' says Lib.

It's an antiques shop—T.S. Crispin's. Wait a second.

'Here,' says Lib. She walks up to the shop and points at a shiny gold plaque on the wall by the door.

IN MEMORY OF GIZMO—HERO DOG

My vision goes swimmy, my chin wobbles. 'Pretty nice, eh?' says Lib. I try to reply but my voice is too choked.

I can't take my eyes off the plaque. It's a permanent reminder that Gizmo was here. And that he was the best.

Chapter Forty-Four

We're sitting on top of the hill, looking out at the town. The roads are busy with people coming home from work. I'm holding my official Gizmo calendar. Lib got it printed at a shop in town. It's strange to see him looking so happy and goofy. How quickly things can change.

'Feels weird, doesn't it?' says Lib, nodding at the town below us. 'When something happens that completely knocks your world on its bum and life just goes on as normal. It's like you want to stop people and say, "How can you be nipping to the shops for a carton of milk when THIS has happened?"' She stops and sighs, picking at the grass. 'But it just does, you know?'

Somewhere further down the hill, a man chucks a tennis ball for his dog, who goes tearing after it like his life depends on it. Just like Gizmo used to.

'What do you think happens?' I ask.

'I think the dog will probably bring the ball back and the bloke will chuck it again,' Lib replies.

'No, I mean when you die.'

Lib shrugs. 'No idea. Mum always used to tell me my nan became a big star in the sky when she died, but even back then I thought that was a load of old rubbish.'

I look up at the clouds as if I'm expecting to see Gizmo smiling back at me like Mufasa. 'Yeah, seems far-fetched.'

'I don't know now though,' says Lib. 'See, I was watching this programme about space the other week and this professor guy said something similar and it was a hundred per cent true.'

'What do you mean?'

'Well basically, he reckons we're all made of tiny atoms that come from space, all the way back from the Big Bang, and after we die, the atoms go back out into the universe to become other stuff. So yeah, Nan might be a bit of a star. She also might be a turnip or Mr Brandrick's undercrackers, but you get what I mean.'

I laugh, which feels weird because I can't remember the last time that happened.

'It's a bit like this,' she goes on, filling her hand with lots of tiny pieces of grass and moving them around. 'The universe is just a big soup of atoms swishing around.' She starts putting some of the pieces together in the middle of her hand. 'But one day, against all the odds, and I'm talking billions and trillions to one, some of those atoms stuck together and became Gizmo for a bit, before going on their merry way.' She holds out her hand and blows the pieces of grass away. We watch them disperse, some floating up into the air and some settling back down on the ground. 'We are so lucky to have been here to see it.'

It's mad, really. Mum, Dad, and Rosa have all tried to make me feel better about Gizmo dying but Lib is the one who has done the best. She makes it sound so beautiful.

'Thank you,' I croak.

Lib smiles and squeezes my shoulders. 'We all have to go back into the universe sometime, but if you think about it, Gizmo went in the best way possible. He saved his best friend, brought down some bad guys, then had one of the best times of his life at the beach, before slipping away quietly, nice and warm and wrapped up, surrounded by his family who loved him. You couldn't ask for better than that.'

We sit for a while longer before Lib has to go home. She says all the attention from the press has shamed the council into giving Lib and her mum more help. She won't have to work now, but she's already had some offers to do freelance dog training. She says Rosa was brilliant, too, which is annoying because maybe I'm going to have to admit she's not as bad as I thought.

Lib walks me home. 'So, you glad you came out, George?'

I nod. 'Thank you.'

Lib lightly thumps my arm. 'Any time. Seriously.'

We stand outside my house for a few seconds, then Lib gets a piece of paper out of her pocket. 'Actually, George. I've got something else for you.'

It's a piece of lined paper, folded over so I can't see what's written on it. 'I know you were writing Gizmo's autobiography, and I was sitting up last night thinking about you and . . .' She hands it over to me. 'I had a go at writing the last chapter.' I go to open it but she stops me. 'No, wait until I'm gone. And, like, you don't have to use it. I just thought you might . . . I'll shut up. See you later, George!'

And with that, she leaves. I put the paper in my pocket and go inside. I'll read it later.

When I open the door, an unfamiliar smell hits me in the face. Pizza! And chips! Mum peers around the corner, smiling. 'Let's forget the diet, eh?'

I sit down at the table, my mouth watering like

mad. Gizmo would have loved this.

'Not in here,' says Mum. 'Tonight, we dine in the theatre!'

Huh?

'The living room. Thought we could watch a film together. Your choice. Not horror, though. I've had enough scares to last me a lifetime.'

I can't believe what I'm hearing. Eating dinner on the settee has been unheard of since Dad left.

I go into the living room and fire up Netflix. I pick a comedy, something we'll both like. I'm about to press play when my phone vibrates. A text from Matt? Here we go.

Hope you're OK.

I don't know how to respond to that. I'll think about it for a while.

Mum walks in with two plates stacked high with pepperoni pizza slices and thick chips.

'Oh, so many carbs,' says Mum as she plonks herself down next to me. She takes a bite of the pizza and her eyes roll back in her head. 'This is so good, it should be illegal.'

We watch the movie and Mum laughs a lot and sometimes remembers to tut afterwards if the joke was a bit rude. It reminds me that things are probably going to be OK. Don't get me wrong, I'll be sad for a long time and there'll probably always be a bit of me that's sad. But life will go on and I am a better, braver person for having known Gizmo. I look at the photo of him on the mantelpiece and smile. Whenever I feel too scared to do something, I'll think of him and power through. And in that way, he'll always be with me.

Gizmo's Final Chapter

So now I'm gone. Zooming across the universe having all kinds of wild adventures among the stars. I'm sad to leave Earth behind, but the galaxy needs me.

Even though I was only there for fourteen years (roughly seventy-eight in dog years) I will always look back on them with love and fondness. George was the very best friend I could have wished for and he gave me the greatest life. I did absolutely everything a dog could hope to do and had tons of fun and it's all thanks to him. We were together from the second Mum and Dad brought him home until I finally blasted off from Golden Beach.

George has no idea how brilliant he is and how many people love him and need him, but hopefully one day he'll realize. Thanks for everything, pal. It was amazing.

Anyway, it's time for me to say goodbye. At least for now. I was Gizmo the Wonder Dog: friend to all (except Reginald), crime-fighter, chaser of squirrels, and lover of Jammie Dodgers. But most of all, I was a very good boy.

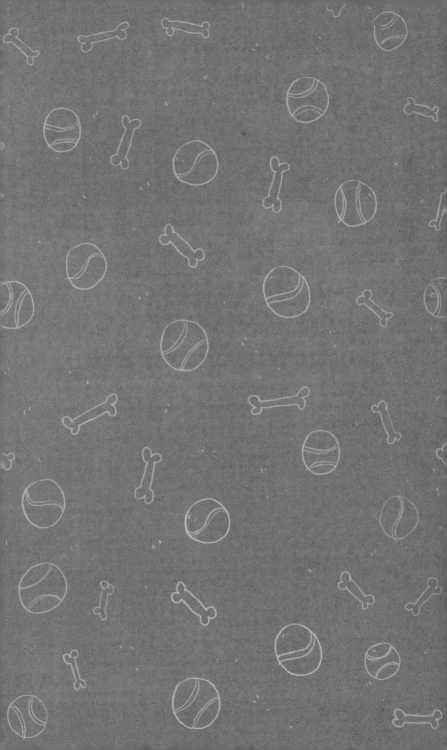

ABOUT THE AUTHOR

As well as writing books, Ben Davis has had a variety of jobs, including joke writer, library assistant, and postman. Writing books has proven the most fun.

Ben lives in Tamworth, Staffordshire, and in his spare time enjoys rock climbing, white water rafting, and pretending to have adventurous hobbies.

ACKNOWLEDGEMENTS

As something of a dog person, I've always wanted to write a book about man's best friend, so I've enjoyed every minute of *What's That in Dog Years?*

Now, if you'll excuse me sounding like I've won an Oscar, there are a number of people I want to thank.

- My long-suffering agent, Penny Holroyde.
- Everyone at OUP, especially Kathy Webb and Gillian Sore, who helped give shape to my jumbled-up idea about a poorly dog.
- My old mucker Amy Millard for her invaluable dog grooming advice.
- Hester for her endless patience and Dougie for his endless kicks to the head.
- All the lovely doggos out there. You're very good. Yes you are, yes you are.